Alice-Miranda
in Japan

Books by Jacqueline Harvey

Alice-Miranda at School
Alice-Miranda on Holiday
Alice-Miranda Takes the Lead
Alice-Miranda at Sea
Alice-Miranda in New York
Alice-Miranda Shows the Way
Alice-Miranda in Paris
Alice-Miranda Shines Bright

Clementine Rose and the Surprise Visitor
Clementine Rose and the Pet Day Disaster
Clementine Rose and the Perfect Present
Clementine Rose and the Farm Fiasco

Alice-Miranda in Japan

Jacqueline Harvey

RANDOM HOUSE AUSTRALIA

Alice-Miranda in Japan was developed as part of a Creative Time Residential Fellowship provided by the May Gibbs Children's Literature Trust.

A Random House book
Published by Random House Australia Pty Ltd
Level 3, 100 Pacific Highway, North Sydney NSW 2060
www.randomhouse.com.au

First published by Random House Australia in 2014

National Library of Australia
Cataloguing-in-Publication Entry

Author: Harvey, Jacqueline
Title: Alice-Miranda in Japan/Jacqueline Harvey
ISBN: 978 1 74275 759 9 (paperback)
Series: Harvey, Jacqueline. Alice-Miranda; 9
Target audience: For primary school age
Subjects: Vacations – Japan – fiction
          Friendships – fiction
Dewey number: A823.4

Cover and internal illustrations by J.Yi
Cover design by Mathematics www.xy-1.com
Internal design by Midland Typesetters, Australia
Typeset in 13/18 pt Adobe Garamond by Midland Typesetters, Australia
Printed in Australia by Griffin Press, an accredited ISO AS/NZS 14001:2004 Environmental Management System printer

Random House Australia uses papers that are natural, renewable and recyclable products and made from wood grown in sustainable forests. The logging and manufacturing processes are expected to conform to the environmental regulations of the country of origin.

For Ian and Sandy

*Thank you to Louisa Chen for her advice on
the Japanese translations*

Glossary of Japanese terms

arigatou	thank you
arigatou gozaimasu	thank you very much
daifuku	rice cake stuffed with bean curd
geta	Japanese wooden sandals
hai	yes
ikebana	art of flower arranging
kawaii	cute, adorable, charming
kimono	a long, loose robe with wide sleeves and tied with a sash, originally worn as a formal garment in Japan
konbanwa	good evening
konnichiwa	good afternoon
koto	13-stringed Japanese zither (instrument)
kuroozudo	closed (shop closed)
momonga	Japanese dwarf flying squirrel
namae	name
obaasan	grandmother (also used to address older women)
ohayou/ohayou gozaimasu	good morning

oishii	delicious
ojiisan	grandfather (also used to address older men)
onsen	hot spring bath
ryokan	traditional inn
-san	a respectful term added to the end of a person's name. Similar to saying Mr or Mrs
sayonara	goodbye
shoji	wooden frame covered in rice paper and used as a room divider
sumimasen	I'm sorry, excuse me
tamagoyaki	rolled omelette
tatami	straw mat flooring
watashi wa Alice-Miranda *desu*	my name is Alice-Miranda
yoku dekimashita	well done/good job
yukata	a cotton robe similar to a kimono, but less formal

Chapter 1

The young girl wove her way through the surging crowd. *'Sumimasen,'* she muttered over and over, apologising to each person she bumped into. She scanned the street, checking to see if she was still being followed, and pulled her baseball cap lower. She wondered if the city was always like this, with so many people in a hurry to be somewhere else.

Up ahead she spied a small group of students in black and white uniforms, long socks and gym shoes. They were talking excitedly and above the din she heard one of them say 'subway'. Her heart beat faster as she scurried to keep up, hoping they would lead her there.

The students walked several blocks then rushed downstairs into a labyrinth of tunnels, where they disappeared into a tangled mass of people.

The girl wanted to stop; to look at the address and find a map, but she was dragged along in the current of commuters and soon became pinned against a barrier. A strange smell filled the air. Sharp and tangy, it was like nothing she'd experienced before. Her stomach clenched and she wondered if it was the unpleasant odour or hunger pangs or maybe just fear.

She looked left and right, unsure of how to make the gate open. Tickets snapped in and out beside her. She was trapped.

An angry voice shouted, telling her to hurry up. A man prodded her in the back. Her mind raced. She saw her opportunity, dropped to her knees and crawled under the turnstile. Then she ran for it, pushing through the mob and forcing her way onto the waiting train. The doors slid shut and the train surged forward. She willed herself to be invisible, slipping into the corner of the carriage where, finally, she breathed.

Chapter 2

Hamish McLoughlin-McTavish glanced in the rear-vision mirror before adjusting the volume control. 'Okay, girls, this is it. Last song before we drop Alice-Miranda off.'

Millie counted them in, 'Two, three, four . . .'

Alice-Miranda and Jacinta swayed in time with the beat, clicking their fingers. Millie was sitting in the middle of the back seat using a banana as a microphone. Together the trio belted out an enthusiastic rendition of 'Mamma Mia'.

Hamish and his wife, Pippa, smiled at one another. The children had certainly kept them entertained for the past couple of weeks.

The four-wheel drive whizzed along the country lane before slowing and turning left into the estate. They passed the pretty gatehouse where Mr and Mrs Greening lived, and drove through the elaborate iron gates that led up to Highton Hall. The girls' song ended triumphantly just as Hamish pulled up outside the kitchen door at the side of the mansion.

He turned off the ignition and glanced around at the back seat. 'Well, that's it. Holiday's over.'

'Noooo,' Jacinta wailed. 'I want to go back to the caravan.'

Millie looked at her friend in amazement. 'Seriously? I never thought *those* words would come out of your mouth.'

'It's true. That was the best holiday ever,' said Jacinta.

'It was a pleasure to have you,' Hamish said, grinning.

Millie smiled to herself. That was another sentence she had never expected to hear. But Jacinta had changed a lot in the past year, and Millie had been glad when the girl agreed to holiday with Millie's family at their caravan on the coast. Sloane had been invited too but her parents had insisted she spend the holidays at home in Spain, much to Sloane's disappointment.

Cecelia Highton-Smith burst out of the kitchen door and scurried down the porch steps. 'Hello darlings!'

'Mummy! We had the best time,' Alice-Miranda exclaimed as she opened the door and leapt into her mother's outstretched arms. She squeezed the woman tight and pecked her cheek. 'Is Daddy home?'

'Yes, he's in the study finishing up some phone calls. He'll be out soon.'

Millie scrambled out of the car and Jacinta followed. Alice-Miranda wriggled from her mother's grasp and slipped to the ground.

'Hello Millie, how was it?' Cecelia asked.

Millie gave Cecelia a hug. 'It was great.'

'And what about you, Jacinta?' Cecelia hugged her too.

'I loved it,' Jacinta smiled.

'Well, you all look wonderful,' Cecelia said. She took note of Millie's sun-kissed freckles and Jacinta's blonder than usual hair.

Pippa hopped out of the car and kissed Cecelia on both cheeks. 'Hello there.' Hamish emerged from the driver's seat looking just as relaxed as his wife. He walked around and greeted Cecelia in the same way.

'How about a cup of tea?' Cecelia asked. 'I thought you might like something before you head off.'

Hamish nodded. 'Wonderful. I'm feeling quite parched after all that singing.'

'Singing?' Cecelia's forehead wrinkled. 'I can't wait to hear about that. And before you ask, girls, Mrs Oliver has made something extra-special for your afternoon tea.'

'Is it devil's food cake?' Alice-Miranda asked.

'No, I hope it's heaven cake,' said Jacinta, whose stomach grumbled right on cue.

Alice-Miranda shook her head. 'I doubt it. Mrs Greening doesn't share that recipe with anyone.'

'I'm not entirely sure what it is, but something in the kitchen smells delicious,' Cecelia said.

'You ladies go inside and I'll get Alice-Miranda's bag,' said Hamish, as he opened the car's tailgate.

'Thank you,' Alice-Miranda called. She motioned to her friends. 'Come on!' The girls raced up the steps and disappeared into the cavernous kitchen.

'They seem a happy bunch,' Cecelia said. 'And you two actually look as if you've had a holiday.'

'Must have been all that sea air,' said Pippa. She linked arms with Cecelia and the two women followed the children inside.

✦

Dolly Oliver bustled out of the pantry and was almost bowled over by Alice-Miranda and her friends.

'Hello there, darling girl!' said Dolly in her lilting Irish brogue. She enveloped Alice-Miranda in a warm embrace, then stepped back and looked at Millie and Jacinta. 'How was it? Did you have a good holiday?'

The children nodded furiously.

'We had the most wonderful time and I can't wait to tell you all about it,' said Alice-Miranda. She raised her nose into the air. 'But what is that delicious smell?'

'You can find out in just a minute. I was about to put the kettle on. Why don't you run along and wash your hands, and then you can come and set the table for me,' said Dolly.

The children rushed through the side sitting room to the downstairs bathroom, and reappeared moments later, ready to help.

'Where's Shilly?' Alice-Miranda asked, referring to the family's resident housekeeper.

'She's taken a few days off to see her sister,' Mrs Oliver explained. 'And not before time. That woman works far too hard.'

'Oh, I'm glad she's having a break,' said Alice-Miranda.

In just a few minutes the three girls, plus Cecelia, Pippa and Hamish, were sitting at the scrubbed pine table with Mrs Oliver's treats taking centre stage. An enormous almond cake sat atop a crystal stand surrounded by a kaleidoscope of chocolate, strawberry, pistachio and caramel macarons.

'These are amazing,' Millie said. A shower of green meringue sputtered from her lips.

'Manners, Millie!' her mother scolded.

'Sorry,' Millie mumbled and wiped her mouth.

'Dolly, please join us,' said Cecelia. 'I wonder where Hugh has got to.'

Just as Cecelia spoke, her husband snuck up behind her and leaned forward to steal a bite of the macaron she was holding.

Cecelia jumped. 'Hugh! You naughty thing.'

The girls laughed.

'I thought I heard some elephants in the house,' Hugh teased.

'Daddy!' Alice-Miranda sprang from her seat and ran to her father, who scooped her up. She kissed him loudly on the cheek and hugged him tightly.

'Now that's what I call a greeting.' Hugh carried his daughter across the room, set her back down in her seat and greeted the others around the table. 'So what mischief did you get up to at the beach, girls?'

'Oh no, there was no mischief,' Alice-Miranda replied, glancing at Millie and Jacinta with a little grin.

'Well, Jacinta *did* shake sand all over Aunt Violet,' Millie said.

'I did not!' Jacinta protested.

Millie gave her friend a meaningful look.

'Not on purpose,' Jacinta added.

'Who's Aunt Violet?' Hugh asked.

'An old lady we met at the beach. She was there with her great-niece, a gorgeous little girl called Clementine Rose. And it was such a coincidence – they live in Penberthy Floss and Clementine is a good friend of Poppy's,' Alice-Miranda explained.

'And there was an old man called Uncle Digby

with them and Clemmie's mother, Clarissa,' Millie continued.

'Do you mean Clarissa Appleby?' Cecelia asked.

Alice-Miranda nodded. 'Do you know her?'

'Not really. Your grandparents were friends with her parents but they drifted apart over time. I suspect it had something to do with the younger sister, Violet.'

Jacinta grimaced. 'Aunt Violet's not young any more. She's wrinkly like a prune and she hardly ever smiles — although she does wear stylish clothes for someone so ancient.'

'I liked her,' Millie said. 'She reminded me of an old lady version of you.'

Jacinta's mouth fell open. 'I hope not. She was crabby.'

'And . . .?' Millie teased.

'Come on, Millie, be nice,' said Hamish.

'What else did you get up to, other than upsetting old ladies?' Hugh asked.

The girls regaled everyone with tales of building giant sandcastles on the beach, regular visits to the ice-cream parlour and swimming in the chilly water. They'd dug for pippies and gone fishing on the pier, although their catch was less than impressive, yielding a puffer fish and a small stingray.

'We had to buy fish and chips from Mr Alessi,' Alice-Miranda explained. 'We didn't catch anything that we could eat.'

'I don't know, I offered to cook that puffer fish but you all turned your noses up,' Hamish said with a wink.

Millie rolled her eyes. 'That's because it was poisonous, Dad.'

The telephone rang. Dolly Oliver hurried from the room and was gone for quite some time. When she finally returned there was a strange grin on her face.

Hugh Kennington-Jones gave her a quizzical look. 'What was that about, Dolly? Why are you looking so pleased with yourself?'

'Was it Grandpa?' Millie asked. Mrs Oliver and Millie's grandfather had struck up a very close friendship over the past year and Millie secretly hoped they might marry one day.

'No. It was a representative of the Japanese Ministry for Invention and Innovation,' Dolly replied with a shake of her head.

'That's intriguing,' said Hugh. 'And what exactly did they want?'

'It's all a bit overwhelming,' she said slowly.

Hugh stood up. 'Come and sit down and I'll pour you some fresh tea.' He thought Dolly looked a little wobbly, which was most unusual. The woman was unshakable, from her sensible navy court shoes to her immovable brown curls.

All eyes were focused on Mrs Oliver.

'Come on, then – don't keep us in suspense,' said Cecelia.

'Well . . . It seems that they knew about the success of my Just Add Water foods and they've invited me to speak at a conference next week in Tokyo,' Dolly explained. 'It all seems rather last minute. I suspect they must have had someone pull out. Why would they ask me?'

A cacophony of support echoed around the room.

Dolly shook her head. 'I . . . I can't go, of course. Not with Alice-Miranda home and Shilly away. There's far too much to be done here.'

Hugh Kennington-Jones tapped his forefinger against his mouth.

Alice-Miranda noticed his thoughtful expression. 'What are you thinking, Daddy?'

'I'm thinking that this is perfect,' he replied.

Cecelia grinned at her husband. 'Yes, of course it is.'

'What's perfect, Mummy?' Alice-Miranda asked.

'Dolly's timing. Your father and I were saying this morning that Highton's has been looking at some new suppliers in Japan, and Charlotte and I were discussing the prospect of sending Rosie Hunter there on assignment to write about the Japanese fashion scene. We could all go and make a holiday of it,' said Cecelia, smiling at Hugh.

Jacinta looked at Millie and Alice-Miranda, the colour draining from her face. She'd confided to her friends while they were away about her mother's new job – but what if Hugh and Cecelia still didn't know who Rosie Hunter really was?

Alice-Miranda bit her lip. 'What about Aunty Gee? I thought I was supposed to be spending some time with her these holidays.'

'I'm sorry, darling, but she telephoned last week when you were away to say that she's been caught up with state matters and your visit will have to wait until half-term. She sounded terribly disappointed.'

'She's not the only one,' Jacinta said, frowning. 'I've been looking forward to a trip to Aunty Gee's palace.'

'What makes you think you'd be invited?' Millie asked.

'Well, I was hoping . . .' Jacinta replied.

'This could be a fun second choice,' Hugh said. 'I know it's only with us boring oldies and it's not to a palace, but I'm sure there will be plenty to see.' He looked at Hamish and Pippa. 'Do you have any plans for the next couple of weeks?'

'Afraid so. I've got some work to do on the farm that just won't wait,' Hamish replied.

'And my locum is going on holidays as soon as we get home,' Pippa added. 'I'll be running the surgery. Can't leave all those animals without a local vet.'

'What about Millie?' Hugh asked.

'I don't know – what do you think, Millie?' Hamish looked across the table at his flame-haired daughter.

Millie was confused. 'About what?'

'Would you like to come to Japan?' Hugh asked.

Millie's eyes almost popped out of her head. 'Are you serious?'

'Yes, of course – if it's all right with your parents?' Hugh looked at Hamish and Pippa, who both nodded.

'Yes, yes, yes!' Millie jumped up and hugged Alice-Miranda.

Jacinta's face fell and she began to pick at the skin around her fingernails.

Hugh noticed the girl's glum expression. 'Of course, you'll be coming too, Jacinta.'

She looked up. 'What did you say?'

'I said that of course you'll be joining us. I don't imagine your mother will leave you at home if she takes the assignment,' Hugh said with a wink.

'But how did you know about Mummy?' Jacinta asked, wide-eyed.

Cecelia looked at the girl. 'Darling, after Paris, Charlotte and I had our suspicions, and then your mother came over while you were away and confessed all. She's brilliant and we're so pleased that she's Rosie Hunter. You must be very proud.'

Jacinta nodded and smiled. 'I couldn't believe it when she first told me, and I wondered if she'd get into trouble, but Mummy said that lots of people write under another name.'

Hamish grinned at his wife. 'Well, Pip, I think our caravan holiday has just slipped out of first place.'

'No,' Jacinta said abruptly and stared across the table at the couple. 'It's still the best holiday ever. At home, that is. And this is going to be the best trip away.'

15

'Well, that's that. Cee, you'd better call Ambrosia and check with her. And why don't you see if Charlotte and Lawrence are free to join us for a few days? Isn't Lucas with them at the moment?' Hugh asked.

'Oh, yes,' Jacinta sighed. 'That's a great idea.'

Everyone else laughed.

'What?' the girl asked, bewildered.

'Gosh, you're thick sometimes,' Millie teased.

'Dolly, telephone the Ministry and tell them you'd be delighted to accept their invitation and I'll see to the accommodation,' Hugh said.

Alice-Miranda looked at Millie and Jacinta. Their smiles couldn't have been any bigger.

Chapter 3

The girl huddled under the yellow glow of the street lamp. She pulled the diary from her dark blue backpack and stared at its pretty cover, her fingers tracing the embossed design. She imagined her mother's hand doing the same thing. Kiko couldn't believe how easy it had been to escape. Perhaps her mother was guiding her. She flipped open the pages to the address she had marked and wondered if it was close by. The subway had been a mistake. She'd had no time to check whether she was on the right line, but she hoped she'd at least travelled in the right direction. Now it was dark, her stomach was grumbling and she was horribly lost.

She put the book away and reached into her pocket, checking that the necklace was still safe. In the distance she could see a huge gate with a low-slung bell and, further on, two rows of shops with customers wandering from side to side. The smell of noodles and *yakitori* filled the air. She gathered her belongings and walked into the market, hoping she would find someone who could help.

'Kiko!' a razor-sharp voice called from inside one of the shops.

The girl jumped. She spun around, scanning the street. Who was calling her?

Seconds later, a small child – no older than five or six – raced out of a souvenir shop and into the store directly opposite.

'Kiko, I told you to stay here. You will get lost,' a young woman scolded the child, who began to cry.

The girl's courage deserted her and she scurried along the lane, passing under another gate, this time with a giant lantern hanging from the rafters. It looked strangely familiar and Kiko wondered if she had been there before. She tried to focus a cloudy memory but it was too long ago.

In front of her was a temple. Red columns rose up to meet the flared roof. She walked up the steps and saw a sign across the doors. *Kuroozudo.* She was tempted to try the door just in case someone had forgotten to lock it. Maybe later.

The streets were still busy but it was nothing like the crowds she'd encountered earlier. The narrow lanes were like an ancient patchwork, bordered by shops and timber houses. A siren wailed in the distance. Kiko held her breath while her heart thumped like a drum. She scurried down an alley and stopped in the relative safety of a darkened doorway. Tomorrow she would find her way to her grandparents' house. But for now she crouched and hoped that somehow she might fall asleep. Life was always better in her dreams.

Hours later, Kiko was dozing when the door opened. She fell backwards, landing on a tiny pair of feet.

The girl was jolted awake. 'Ahh!'

'What are you doing in my doorway?' a shrill voice demanded.

'I . . . I,' Kiko began. She rolled over and leapt up. The old woman standing in the doorway thrust a plastic bag into Kiko's hand. 'Huh, that's okay. If you want to sleep in my doorway, you can take my rubbish. Save me the walk.'

Kiko held the bag and wondered what she should do next.

'Well, what are you doing? You blind or something?'

The girl shook her head.

'The garbage bin is over there.' The woman pointed a gnarled finger at the industrial bin on the other side of the lane.

Kiko hesitated.

'Do you want a written invitation? I'm too busy for that,' the woman snorted.

Kiko walked to the bin. She was about to throw the bag away when she noticed a pleasant smell coming from inside it. She peered in at a mixture of chicken bones and rice. Her stomach let out a strangled whine.

'Why are you taking so long?' the woman demanded. 'What are you doing over there?'

Kiko reluctantly dropped the bag over the edge of the dumpster.

'Why are you sleeping in my doorway? Haven't you got a home?' the woman asked.

Kiko froze.

'Come here, I want to look at you.'

Kiko was about to run when she realised that she'd left her backpack in the doorway and it was now wedged under the woman's foot. She gulped and walked towards the light. The woman wore a grey smock dress, which swamped her tiny frame. There was a red scarf around her neck and knitted slippers on her feet. Her face was wrinkled like a currant and the skin under her cloudy eyes sagged like tea bags. Her thinning hair stuck out like straw and was the colour of snow. Kiko was at least an inch taller than her.

'Come closer.'

Kiko stepped forward and stared at the ground. The woman squinted and pressed her nose against Kiko's. Then she ran her gnarled hands over the girl's face and neck, her fingers drawing the image of the child. Kiko's long hair was plaited tightly and hidden beneath a baseball cap.

She could have run. The woman was frail and wouldn't stand a chance against a healthy eleven-year-old. But Kiko's feet felt as if they were set in concrete and she couldn't leave the diary behind.

'Why are you here, boy?' the old woman demanded. 'What's your name?'

Kiko said nothing.

'Are you stupid or something?'

Kiko felt the heat rising in her neck. She hated that word. She had heard it too many times before.

'Yoshi.' The name tumbled out. He was a character in a book she had read.

'Where are your parents?'

Kiko's face fell.

'Are they dead?' the woman asked.

Kiko remained silent but nodded her head ever so slightly.

'I need a helper. Do you want to stay here? I'll give you food and a bed and you'll help me. Okay?'

Kiko gulped.

'I suppose you will have to go to school, but we can work that out later. You can go with fat boy.'

Kiko wondered who that was. But just the thought of school made her heart soar.

'Good, that's settled. You stay here and I will look after you. But mostly you will look after me. Okay? Okay.' Then the woman laughed and put her hands on Kiko's shoulders. 'Well, boy, are you coming or not? I haven't got all night. I know I look good but I am tired.' She gave Kiko a shrewd look. 'Pretend I'm your granny. You can call me Obaasan.'

Kiko allowed herself to be propelled inside the house. She didn't feel her necklace fall from her pocket, or see the tall man with the pockmarked face walking down the alley towards the house. He picked up the necklace, looked around, and shoved it into his pocket.

Chapter 4

Two days after returning from their seaside holiday, Alice-Miranda, Millie and Jacinta were on their way to Tokyo, along with Ambrosia Headlington-Bear, Alice-Miranda's parents and Mrs Oliver.

Ambrosia had been thrilled to learn of her special assignment and had her bags packed in no time flat. She was glad that she'd come clean with Cecelia and Hugh about her alter ego, Rosie Hunter, but she was still planning to stick with the name for work. She was enjoying having a slightly mysterious side to her life.

The group would be staying in Tokyo for the first week, before venturing out of the city the week after to explore some of the charming villages and towns further afield. Charlotte and Lawrence and Lawrence's son, Lucas, would be joining them in a couple of days.

'So, what do you girls want to see in Tokyo?' Hugh asked. He'd joined the children for their inflight meal. The Highton's private jet was configured so that four passengers could sit facing one another with a table between them. There were another four seats across the aisle where Alice-Miranda's mother, Mrs Oliver and Ambrosia were sitting. Further along, a lounge area faced inwards.

'It would be fun to go on the bullet train,' Jacinta said.

Millie nodded. 'They call it the Shinkansen and it goes over three hundred kilometres an hour.'

Hugh nodded. 'That's how we're getting to the mountains.'

'Cool,' Millie said. 'What would you like to do, Alice-Miranda?'

'I read something about the Imperial Palace. I'm not sure if it's open to the public but that would be amazing to see.'

'We can visit the gardens, sweetheart, but the palace is off limits, I'm afraid,' Hugh said.

'What are we doing tomorrow, Daddy?' the child asked.

'Well, your mother and Ambrosia have meetings and Mrs Oliver will be at her conference, so I thought we could explore the local area around the inn. There's a stunning temple close by.'

The girls nodded in agreement as the young flight attendant cleared their plates.

An hour later, as the jet began its descent towards the runway at Narita airport, Millie and Jacinta jostled to see out of the window. Hugh had gone to sit with Cecelia in the lounge and Mrs Oliver was strapped in opposite Ambrosia on the other side of the aisle. Thousands of lights twinkled below them.

'Wow! Tokyo is huge,' Jacinta gasped. 'It looks like fairyland.'

'It says here that there are thirteen-point-two *million* people living in the city,' said Millie, tapping her finger on the page. 'That's about ten million more than Paris and we thought *that* was big.'

As soon as Millie's grandfather had learned that she was off on another adventure, he'd gone straight out and bought her a new guidebook. The Paris version had been a great success. He also wanted an excuse to see Mrs Oliver before she headed off, and delivering the book to Millie at Highton Hall was just the thing.

Jacinta shot Millie a dubious look. 'Are you going to bore us to death with lots of irritating facts again?'

'I think it's wonderful that Millie likes to find out about things. Her knowledge of Paris on our school trip was fantastic,' said Alice-Miranda, defending her friend. 'She knew loads more than the rest of us.'

'Yes, I agree, Alice-Miranda,' said Ambrosia. She scowled at her daughter from the other side of the aisle. 'I think it will come in very handy. The only time I've been here before was with your father on a business trip, and I don't remember seeing anything other than the inside of the hotel. I was so scared of getting lost, I didn't venture out at all. But I'm looking forward to experiencing Japan properly this time.'

'It's a pity that none of us speaks the language,' Alice-Miranda said. 'It would make life much easier.'

Dolly Oliver was jotting notes for her conference presentation. She glanced up on hearing the conversation. She wished she'd had more time to work on her latest invention before the trip, but at least she could trial it while they were here – provided she had privacy. It wasn't ready for general consumption. Nevertheless, she was excited about the prospect of perfecting her discovery. After more years fiddling and faddling than she cared to remember, she'd hit on something quite extraordinary. Possibly even more extraordinary than her Just Add Water food. She opened the bulging handbag on the seat beside her and peered at the pill case inside. For now, it would remain her secret.

Soon enough, the eager travellers were off the plane and in a limousine, weaving their way through the city.

'Daddy, where are we staying?' Alice-Miranda asked. She was staring out the window at the tall buildings with their enormous electronic billboards, and the waves of people moving along the footpaths.

'Your mother and I decided that we'd like you all to have an authentic Japanese experience, so we've opted for a small *ryokan*.'

'What's that?' Jacinta asked.

'It's a traditional inn,' Cecelia explained.

'It says here,' Millie read from her guidebook, 'that *ryokans* will provide travellers with a taste of the real Japan. It also says that you have to sleep on futons on the *tatami* mats.'

Jacinta's lip curled. 'On the floor?'

'Don't worry. I'm sure it won't be any different to being at the caravan and sleeping on the camp beds in the annexe,' Millie said.

'Let me see that.' Jacinta reached for Millie's guidebook. It was open to a photograph of a futon. 'Seriously, it's on the floor!'

Millie let out an exasperated sigh.

'Which is exactly why I'll be leaving you to your fun,' Dolly said, raising her eyebrows.

'What do you mean?' Alice-Miranda asked.

'Dolly's staying at the hotel where her conference is on,' Hugh explained. 'At least until we can coax her to come back to us at the end of the week.'

'You make me sound like a spoilsport, sir, but I'm just a little worried about my back seizing up. I'm not as young as I once was,' Dolly said.

Alice-Miranda smiled at the woman. 'Staying at the hotel makes perfect sense.'

'So now you're agreeing that I'm old, are you, miss?' Dolly teased.

'No, of course not, but I imagine you'll want to have time to meet lots of other inventors and scientists.'

Dolly nodded. 'You're right about that, dear.

It's not often you receive an invitation like this. Come to think of it, it's the only time I've had an invitation like this, so I really should make the most of it. There are some very accomplished men and women attending.'

'And you're one of them, of course,' Alice-Miranda said.

'Oh no, I'm just a dabbler, dear,' Dolly protested.

Hugh winked at her. 'A dabbler whose invention is changing the course of history.'

Dolly's cheeks lit up. 'Mr Hugh, I think you're exaggerating again.'

The limousine turned into the entrance of a towering hotel. Dolly said her goodbyes and Cecelia saw her inside, returning after a few minutes. They set off again and soon Alice-Miranda noticed that their surroundings were changing. Although they were still in the centre of the crowded city, this neighbourhood consisted of narrow lanes and low-rise timber houses.

The limousine pulled up outside a dark timber building. A squat stone lantern sat on the edge of the road, illuminating the entrance. A rickshaw leaned against the wall at the end of the slim veranda and pretty paper lanterns danced above.

Hugh helped the driver with the bags. The girls each took care of their own suitcases and followed Cecelia and Ambrosia into a small entrance hall. A shoe cupboard took up the length of one wall. Jacinta looked at the array of footwear in the pigeonholes and the slippers lined up on the floor. 'Do we really have to take our shoes off?'

'Yes, of course,' Millie said, as she stuffed her feet into a pair of satin slippers and put her own shoes away. 'And you have to take the slippers off on the *tatami* and there are special slippers just for the bathroom too.'

'How am I supposed to remember all that?' Jacinta whined. 'And what if you've got smelly feet like Sloane?'

'I suppose they might have a supply of pegs,' said Hugh as he joined the girls.

'What for?' Jacinta asked.

He grinned. 'The noses of the other guests.'

'Oh Daddy, your jokes are getting worse.' Alice-Miranda shook her head but Jacinta laughed.

'Well, Jacinta thinks I'm funny,' Hugh said and winked at the girl.

The group walked into the foyer. It was like nothing the girls had seen before. The walls looked as if they were made of paper and there were dark timber beams lining the ceiling. A glass case opposite the reception desk housed a collection of wooden *kokeshi* dolls, lined up in rows, and several stunning floral arrangements decorated the room.

Cecelia pointed at a striking display of orchids. 'Aren't they lovely? That type of flower arranging is called *ikebana*.'

'They're gorgeous, Mummy.' Alice-Miranda inspected the vase closely. 'Mr Charles loves his orchids and I know he's got some rare beauties growing in the greenhouse at school. I'll have to take some photographs for him.'

A young woman with sparkling brown eyes walked through a door behind the reception desk. She was dressed in the most beautiful pale green kimono. '*Konbanwa*. My name is Aki.' She bowed.

'*Konbanwa*, Aki-san,' Hugh replied and bowed in return.

Cecelia and Ambrosia smiled at the girl too.

'How was your journey, Mr Kennington-Jones?' the girl asked in perfect English.

'Very good, thank you,' Hugh replied. 'But we're glad to be here.'

'I hope that you are happy with the rooms we

have set aside for you.' She smiled and walked out from behind the counter. 'I have one for the three young ladies.' She handed Hugh an engraved key ring. He passed it to Alice-Miranda.

'Look, Daddy, it has our names on it,' she said, beaming.

Aki nodded at her. 'You must be Miss Alice-Miranda.'

'*Hai,*' the child replied. 'It's lovely to meet you, Aki-san.'

'I see you have been practising your Japanese,' the girl replied. 'I am pleased to improve my English too. Perhaps you can help me and I will help you with some lessons in Japanese.'

Alice-Miranda nodded. 'That would be wonderful.'

Aki handed another key to Ambrosia and there was a third one for Hugh and Cecelia. 'I will show you to your rooms,' she said, holding out her hand. 'Please come this way.' Aki walked along a dimly lit hallway then stopped in a doorway. 'This is the breakfast room and is also our restaurant in the evenings. On the other side we have a sitting room. There are some board games that the children might like in the cupboard.'

She continued further down the passage before heading up a dark timber staircase to the first floor. A central hallway divided the rooms left and right. 'This is for Mrs Headlington-Bear.' She slid open the door to reveal a spacious room almost devoid of furniture.

Jacinta poked her head inside. 'Where's the bed?'

'Come and I will show you.' Aki turned and opened the door opposite. 'This is your room. Slippers off, please.'

'The floor feels nice,' Millie said. 'It's *tatami*, isn't it?'

'Yes,' said Aki. 'It's made of thick straw, and we measure the size of a room by how many *tatami* mats fit on the floor.'

'But there are no beds in here either,' Jacinta scoffed. 'How can this be a hotel without any beds?'

'You will see,' Aki said. She opened a small wardrobe and pulled out a thick roll of material, which she unravelled on the floor.

Jacinta thought it looked like a sleeping bag. She plonked herself down, expecting it to be hard. 'Oh, that's really soft! And that duvet is heavenly.' She fluffed it with her hand.

'I am glad it is to your liking,' Aki said.

'Girls, are you happy to get settled while your father and I have a look at our room?' Cecelia asked. Ambrosia had already disappeared into her room across the hallway.

'Of course, Mummy,' Alice-Miranda said, as she pulled another futon from the cupboard.

'This way, please.' Aki motioned at Hugh and Cecelia. She slid the door closed and left the girls alone.

'This room is weird,' Jacinta said, as she walked around. It was a bare space with only a couple of pieces of furniture against the wall. There was a large wardrobe, a low lacquered table holding an arrangement of orchids and nothing else.

'It *is* plain,' Millie agreed.

'I think there's something lovely about how simple it all is,' Alice-Miranda said.

'How will we lay out the beds?' Millie asked. Even with two futons unrolled there was still plenty of space.

'I don't know, but come and have a look at this.' Jacinta had discovered the ensuite through an almost invisible sliding screen.

Alice-Miranda and Millie rushed over to join her.

'That's the cutest thing I've ever seen,' said Alice-Miranda as she looked at the tiny bath in the corner. It was no more than sixty centimetres square.

'I wouldn't even fit into that and I'm a midget,' Millie said.

'I think you must stand up and use this.' Alice-Miranda picked up a shower head attached to a long pipe.

'Check out the toilet.' Jacinta was examining the control panel on the side of the unit. She went to lift the lid and dropped it straight back down. 'Oh yuck, it's warm! Like someone's just been sitting on it.'

'What do you mean, it's warm?' Millie went to touch it too. 'Oh. It must be heated.' Millie lifted the lid and looked inside. 'It's just a normal toilet.'

'Then what does this do?' Jacinta pressed a button and a spurt of warm water shot out of the bowl and hit Millie in the eye.

'Disgusting.' Millie wiped her face. 'What's that for?'

Alice-Miranda giggled. 'I think it's like a bidet.'

'A bid-what? Oh, gross,' Jacinta said as she realised. 'I won't be pushing that button again. What's this one do?'

A blast of warm air escaped from the bowl.

'It's like a hand dryer,' Millie said. 'Except it's for your bottom.'

'I might use that. It feels nice.' Jacinta rubbed her hands together over the top of the toilet bowl. They all laughed.

Cecelia Highton-Smith slid open the girls' door and walked into the room. She could see the three of them gathered in the bathroom. Ambrosia joined her.

'How are you getting on, then?' Cecelia asked.

'Mummy, this toilet is high-tech,' Alice-Miranda said excitedly.

'Yes, you have to expect that in Japan. I remember the first time I came to Tokyo; I was staying in a hotel that had a toilet with more controls than a spaceship. I remember pressing one button and getting the shock of my life,' Cecelia said. 'Anyway, I think you should be brushing your teeth and getting into your pyjamas. It's been a long day and we need to get to bed. Tomorrow you can go exploring.'

The girls bade goodnight to Ambrosia and Cecelia. Hugh popped his head in the door when they were all settled.

Alice-Miranda jumped up out of bed and kissed her father. 'Goodnight, Daddy.'

'Goodnight, darling. Goodnight, Millie and Jacinta.' He flicked off the overhead light.

Within a very short time all three girls were fast asleep.

Chapter 5

A woman glided down a dimly lit hallway. As always, she wore a black suit with a choker of pearls and matching earrings. Her long black tresses were wound into a tight bun at the nape of her neck. The only splashes of colour were the blood-red polish on her fingernails and the slash of crimson across her lips. As she neared the end of the passage, a screen slid open and a man stepped into her path. She bowed deeply and then looked up and whispered, 'How is he today?'

'The same,' the man replied.

'When will things change?' she asked, shaking her head.

'He could go on like this forever,' the man replied. 'And how are you, Hatsuko?'

'I'm fine.' She averted her gaze.

'And Kiko?' he asked.

Hatsuko shrugged.

'She rarely comes out of her room these days,' he said. 'I have not seen her in weeks.'

'I do my best with her,' said Hatsuko.

'You are a good aunt, but you take on far too much of the child's care. We have many who can help.'

'But she is family, Kenzo,' Hatsuko said.

He smiled. 'Your patience is a virtue.'

Hatsuko bowed her head. Kenzo returned the gesture and hurried away.

A sinister smile crept onto the woman's lips. It was true. Her patience would soon be rewarded. In the end, it had been far easier than she could have imagined. The child herself had come up with the plan and all Hatsuko had to do was help her see it through. It was an unexpected bonus that the girl had written a letter explaining her actions. This was now safely tucked away in a drawer in Hatsuko's apartment until it was needed. Who could tell how the girl's father would react to the news? But she would be there to console her brother and convince him to do what was best for everyone. And soon enough she would have what was rightfully hers.

Hatsuko waited until Kenzo's footsteps receded down the corridor, then turned away from the sliding door. She had more important things to do than sit with her melancholy brother. She turned sharply to her left and strode down the narrow corridor. After going down two flights of stairs and unlocking a low door, she entered a small basement room.

Two men in black suits looked up as she entered, and bowed quickly at her.

'What are you doing here?' Hatsuko demanded. The men resembled a pair of naughty schoolboys. There was no way they could have completed their task already. 'Where is she?'

Both men gulped. Yuki cast his eyes to the floor, while Yamato stared at the ceiling, neither of them wanting to speak first.

Hatsuko could feel the heat rising in her body. 'You've lost her, haven't you? Don't just stand there like imbeciles – one of you find your tongue and explain to me!' she hissed.

The taller man, Yuki, straightened and looked ahead, focusing on the blank wall. 'We did not expect her to go to the subway. We followed her, of course, but there were too many people.'

'Too many people – in Tokyo? What a shock! You're more stupid than I ever imagined.'

He cleared his throat. 'Please forgive us. One minute she was there and the next she was gone, like a puff of smoke. We have been searching for hours but there's no sign of her.'

'This child cannot just disappear!' Hatsuko screamed. 'Not until I say so! Who is helping her?'

The men looked at each other and shrugged.

Hatsuko stormed towards the pair. 'Pathetic! Useless!' she shrieked. The men flinched.

Hatsuko stalked back across the room, her mind ticking over. They must find a snow drop in a puddle. A snow drop who wanted nothing more than to melt into the waters around her and disappear forever. Hatsuko smiled to herself. It was a bitter irony. She wanted the same thing for her little snow drop too – but only if she was in control.

'What did she take with her?' Hatsuko strode

back to the men. Their heads were bowed and they dared not look up. 'Surely you know that!' She tipped Yuki's chin upwards and stared into his eyes.

Finally he spoke. 'A backpack with some clothes and her mother's diary.'

The other man looked up. 'And she took the necklace, the one her father gave her.'

'The necklace! But she wasn't wearing it when she left.'

'No. It was in her pocket. I saw her take it out when she was walking,' the other man said.

'So you were that close and still you lost her?'

Both men nodded.

A stifling silence enveloped the room. Hatsuko stared ahead, a frightening smile forming on her lips. 'Oh, this is perfect. I should have known I would have to rely on my own abilities.'

The men wondered what she was talking about. Kiko was still missing and the fact that she had taken a gold necklace and a diary with her was not any help as far as they were concerned.

'Come with me, you idiots,' Hatsuko sighed. She stalked towards the far end of the room and unlocked another door. 'I will show you how to do your jobs.'

Chapter 6

Cecelia Highton-Smith tapped on the girls' door then slid it open and whispered, 'Good morning.' Alice-Miranda, Millie and Jacinta were still asleep on their futons in the middle of the *tatami* floor. Despite starting off in separate corners, they'd somehow wriggled to the centre and were huddled together like caterpillars in their downy cocoons.

Millie was the first to stir. She opened her eyes and stretched her arms above her head.

Cecelia knelt down beside her. 'Hello, sleepyhead.'

'Good morning.' Millie sat up and yawned.

Jacinta was snoring gently: little grunts punctuated by the occasional whistling breath. Alice-Miranda rolled over and rubbed her eyes. 'Hello Mummy. Did we sleep in?'

'No, darling, but I thought I'd better wake you. Breakfast is ready. Why don't you put on your robes and come downstairs,' Cecelia suggested.

'Don't we have to get dressed?' Millie asked.

'No, we can go to breakfast in our *yukatas.*' Cecelia stood up and twirled around in her pretty blue robe. 'It's the thing to do when staying in a *ryokan.*'

'I saw them hanging in the wardrobe. They sort of look like cotton kimonos,' said Alice-Miranda. She stood up and went to get one.

'Jacinta.' Cecelia gently put her hand on the girl's arm.

'You'll never wake her like that. Trust me, she sleeps like a sloth,' Millie said. She leaned over and whispered sharply in Jacinta's ear, 'You're late!'

The girl sat bolt upright. 'What? Sorry, Howie, I didn't hear the bell.' Jacinta scrambled out of bed onto the *tatami.* A few seconds later she looked around, clearly confused, and realised that she wasn't in her dormitory bedroom at all.

Millie laughed.

'Calm down, sweetheart. There's plenty of time,' Cecelia cooed. 'Oh, Millie, that's cruel.'

Jacinta exhaled loudly and glared at Millie. 'Why did you do that?'

'Do what?' Millie replied innocently, batting her eyelashes.

'Come on girls, I'll be back in a few minutes. Just put on your robes and slippers and we'll get something to eat. I don't know about you but I could murder a cup of tea,' Cecelia said and walked out of the room.

✴

In the cosy dining room of the Sadachiyo Ryokan, Alice-Miranda, Millie and Jacinta discovered an interesting selection of food for their breakfast. There was miso soup, rice porridge and even some broiled fish.

Alice-Miranda pointed at one of the plates and smiled at the young girl who was serving them. 'Could you tell me what this is, please?'

'*Tamagoyaki*. I think you would call it an omelette,' the girl explained. She bowed and then retreated from the room.

Jacinta used her chopsticks to pick up what looked like a pink vegetable. She sniffed it and screwed up her nose.

'I think it's a pickle,' said Alice-Miranda.

'Oh, that's disgusting.' Jacinta flung it back into the bowl. 'Yuck!'

'I'll try it.' Millie reached over and popped the vegetable into her mouth. 'It's okay.'

Alice-Miranda tucked into the omelette. 'Oh, that's delicious. Just like Mrs Oliver's.'

'Well, I'm not eating *that*.' Jacinta pointed at two dried fish, whose beady eyes were staring up at her from the plate.

Millie prodded her with a chopstick. 'I think you're going to be starving by the end of the week.'

'I don't care,' Jacinta replied. 'Surely there are some steak restaurants around here somewhere.'

The girls sat together while Cecelia, Hugh and Ambrosia were at another small table on the other side of the room. All of the tables were low and surrounded by cushions for the guests to kneel on. A young couple sat at the far end of the room, and another table was occupied by a family of two parents and a son and daughter.

Millie took a sip of her tea. She spat it out and wiped her mouth on a napkin. 'Yuck!'

'What's the matter?' Alice-Miranda asked.

'What sort of tea is that?' Millie stared into the cup.

'It's green tea,' Alice-Miranda said. She peered into the cup at the cloudy liquid. 'Did you put milk in it?'

'Yes, of course. I always have milk in my tea – and two sugars,' Millie replied.

'No wonder it tastes awful.' Alice-Miranda grinned. 'You're supposed to drink it on its own. I guarantee you'll like it better that way.'

'How was I supposed to know that?' Millie set the cup back down. 'Why did they put milk on the tray?'

'I think it was for the rice porridge,' Alice-Miranda said, casting her eye over the breakfast items. 'I only know about green tea because Mummy's a big fan. I hated it to start with but it's one of those things that the more you try it the more you'll like it – I think. Wait until you have green tea ice-cream.'

Jacinta shuddered. 'That sounds truly –' She stopped as the little girl on the table next to her began to howl.

'What's *this*?' The girl waved a piece of fish in the air. 'And why can't I have a fork? Chopsticks are stupid.'

'Not as stupid as you,' her brother snapped.

'Cadence, stop playing with your food,' her mother whispered. 'Please.' The woman looked over and gave Alice-Miranda and her friends an apologetic smile.

The boy was now flicking grains of rice at his sister and singing a rude song about how smelly her feet were. The father continued to read his book.

Jacinta closed her mouth and picked up her own cup of green tea.

Millie noticed Jacinta's appalled expression and laughed. 'It's like looking in a mirror, isn't it?'

'No,' Jacinta gulped. 'I've changed, and please tell me I was never that bad. Was I?'

Millie grinned.

Hugh Kennington-Jones beckoned for the girls to join them. 'Have you made some new friends?' he asked, peering at the family on the other side of the room.

'No way,' said Jacinta. 'Those children are revolting.'

Millie gave a sly wink. 'Even worse than Jacinta.'

Ambrosia looked up and smiled. 'Really, Millie? Is that possible?'

Jacinta glared at her mother.

'I was just joking, darling. Surely you know that by now.' Ambrosia Headlington-Bear reached out and grabbed Jacinta around the middle, pulling her onto the floor and into her lap.

Jacinta rolled her eyes.

'We should get moving. What about you girls have a quick bath and then you can head off with your father,' Cecelia suggested.

'I think it will be a shower in that funny little tub of ours,' Alice-Miranda replied. 'What are you doing today, Mummy?'

'I'm afraid Ambrosia and I have quite a few meetings scheduled this week but we should be able to catch up for lunches, and I've set aside some time for a few special things.'

'I'm looking forward to having the girls to myself,' Hugh said.

'Have you decided what we're doing, Daddy?' Alice-Miranda asked.

'I'm pretty flexible, but I thought today we could have a look at the Senso-ji Temple, and later in the week we can go to the Imperial Palace gardens, and I thought we might visit the Tokyo Tower too.'

'Maybe we should write a list,' Millie suggested. 'I saw in my guidebook that there's a children's museum. And what about a sumo tournament?'

'Good plan,' said Hugh.

'Sumo? Yuck! Who wants to see fat men in nappies wrestling?' Jacinta screwed up her face.

'Come on, Jacinta, it's not something you see every day,' Hugh grinned. 'And those fellows train really hard, you know. I think it would be fun.'

'Well, you and Millie can go. I'll sit that one out,' Jacinta told her friends.

'All right, girls, off you go and get dressed,' Cecelia said.

The three children scampered upstairs, chatting about the day ahead.

Chapter 7

Kiko opened her eyes and wondered for a moment where she was. She looked up at the shelves lining the room, which were groaning under the weight of hundreds of tiny squirrel figurines.

When she had followed the old woman inside the previous evening, Kiko was surprised to find a giant squirrel, taller than herself, standing guard in the hallway. At the time Kiko had covered her mouth, hiding her smile. She didn't want to disrespect Obaasan's decorating preferences but she had never seen anything like it.

She rolled over on the thin futon that she'd pushed close to the wall. Her backpack and jacket were hidden under the covers. The air inside the house was thick with a smell Kiko didn't recognise and it was far too warm for comfort.

'Boy, where are you?' Obaasan's voice screeched through the wall.

Kiko lay still, her eyes heavy and threatening to close again. She could happily have gone back to her dreams.

The door slid open and the old woman appeared beside her, tapping her foot against Kiko's bottom. 'You get up.' She kicked a little harder. 'The old people are hungry and you are lazy.'

Kiko wondered who these old people were. She was about to sit up when she felt something shift down her back and realised it was her own plaited rope of hair. She snatched up the baseball cap beside her and jammed it onto her head, swiftly tucking the plait underneath. She hoped Obaasan hadn't noticed.

The woman shuffled out and away down the hall. Insults spewed from her lips as she berated Kiko's idleness. Except, of course, that she called her 'boy' and 'Yoshi'.

Kiko hurried to the bathroom, where another shelf of squirrels stared at her with their big brown eyes.

'What are you looking at?' she whispered, then scampered down the hallway in search of Obaasan.

'Yoshi!' the old woman called sharply.

Kiko walked into the kitchen, which was larger than she remembered from the previous evening when the old woman had given her a bowl of noodles. Yet more squirrel figurines were crammed on top of the cabinets. There was a row of medicine bottles too, with labels in large letters. Lined up along a countertop were several trays with bowls of steaming noodles.

'Where have you been, boy? Why do you take so long in the toilet? Are you baking bread in there?' Obaasan wrinkled her nose and squinted at Kiko through thick glasses. 'I hope you washed your hands.'

Kiko nodded.

'Have you got a tongue?' the old woman demanded. 'Never mind. I don't care if you don't speak. Probably better not – then I won't get sick of your voice. Take these.' She pointed at the noodles.

Kiko noticed several pools of broth slopped onto

the trays. She looked around for a napkin or a cloth to mop up.

'What are you waiting for? The old people will starve to death before you get them breakfast,' Obaasan tutted. 'But make sure they go out in order – left to right. Okay?'

Kiko picked up the first tray. She had no idea what the woman meant and she didn't want to ask.

Obaasan pointed. 'Through there. The room on the other side of the hall.'

Kiko hesitated, then pushed her shoulder against the kitchen door and walked through. She pushed against the door on the opposite side of the wide entrance hall and was surprised to see a room full of elderly people sitting around a huge table. She was less surprised to see squirrel figurines lining yet another shelf. Obaasan must have had the biggest collection in the whole of Japan. Kiko was unused to such clutter and she was fascinated to think how long it had taken the woman to amass such a huge number of items. Kiko placed the tray on a side-board and picked up one of the bowls, which she set in front of the woman closest to her.

A man with a shock of white hair shook his head and made a fist. 'No! You always start down there.'

Kiko quickly picked it up again and walked to the far end of the table. She placed the bowl in front of a woman with a long grey plait wound on top of her head. The old woman looked up at Kiko and smiled.

Kiko carried each bowl separately, determined not to spill any of their contents. A few minutes later the door flew open and Obaasan shuffled into the dining room.

'What's taking you so long, boy? He will be dead before he gets his breakfast.' She pointed a knobbly finger at the gentleman sitting opposite her. The old man guffawed and winked at Obaasan.

Kiko gulped and walked faster, aware of the contents of the bowl sploshing over the sides.

'She thinks I'm joking,' Obaasan cackled.

Kiko made several trips back to the kitchen for more noodles. Her own stomach was grumbling. She hoped there would be some food left over.

In the dining room she counted twenty people. Kiko wondered if the place was an inn, but that seemed strange as the clientele were all so old. Most of them looked as if they'd struggle to walk more than a few steps, let alone go travelling. None of them had half the energy of Obaasan and yet she looked older than the lot.

Obasaan reappeared at the doorway. 'Boy, you take the bowls to the kitchen and wash up. I will get the tea.'

Kiko walked carefully back across the hall into the kitchen with a tray of empty dishes, which she deposited next to the sink. She looked around, unsure what to do next. After rummaging about, she found a plug and turned on the taps, then dumped a stack of bowls into the steaming water.

Noodles floated on top and an oily film created kaleidoscopes on the surface. Kiko plunged her hands into the sink and shuddered. The dishes still felt slimy when she put them on the draining board.

Obaasan returned to the kitchen and shuffled past her.

'Good boy. Did you find the detergent and put the leftovers in the bucket?' The old woman squinted. Her nose turned up like a pig's snout every time she did this.

Kiko looked around and saw a plastic bucket adorned with yet another squirrel motif sitting on the bench. Her eyes scanned the open shelves and fell upon a plastic bottle whose label showed a pair of hands amid a froth of bubbles and a sparkling plate.

Obaasan left the room and Kiko quickly started again.

There had still been no offer of food and Kiko was beginning to feel nauseated. She finished her task and waited for the old woman.

Finally Obaasan returned. 'Are you hungry, boy?'

Kiko nodded.

'Then eat!' she exclaimed. 'What do you think I am? Your servant? You are young – you can help yourself. Those people in there, they are so old I think the Buddha is their younger brother.' She cackled at her own joke.

Kiko snatched a clean bowl and filled it with noodles from the stovetop. She sat at the small table in the corner of the room and ate with dainty precision, careful not to spill a drop nor slurp.

'What? You don't like my noodles?' Obaasan sat down with a small cup of tea opposite the girl.

'I . . . I do,' Kiko replied.

'So you have a tongue,' Obaasan said. 'Where are you from, boy?'

Kiko did not answer. She wanted to ask about the address in her mother's diary but it wasn't the right time. Her stomach knotted at the thought of heading back out into the city. There were so many people and yet she was afraid to ask any of them for help.

'Did you run away? Are you in trouble? Do you want to take the old people's money?' Obaasan grinned, revealing a row of stained teeth.

Kiko shook her head vigorously. 'No.' She wondered what the woman was talking about.

'I'm just joking about the old people. That's my job,' she laughed. 'You full?'

'Hai,' Kiko said quietly. She had never met anyone like Obaasan before.

'Good. Now you get to make beds. Save my old back. I'm glad you were asleep on my doorstep, boy. I like you. You're helpful and the washing up is not too bad for the first time,' Obaasan said.

Kiko wondered how she knew it was the first time she'd ever washed up. She'd never made a bed before either but she'd watched it being done and surely it couldn't be too hard. Obaasan shuffled into the hallway and beckoned for Kiko to follow her. The front hall sat perpendicular to a long hallway that ran the width of the building. Obaasan turned left and walked towards a set of stairs at the end of the corridor. Kiko turned and glanced back at the side door where she'd entered the house the night before. She was surprised to see a huge padlock and another bolt protecting it. Kiko gulped. Perhaps it would not be as easy to leave as she'd thought.

Chapter 8

Alice-Miranda stood in a wide promenade bustling with tourists and admired the bold red colour of the temple in front of her. 'It's lovely, isn't it, Daddy?' she asked, squeezing her father's hand.

'Yes, she's not bad for an old girl,' Hugh replied.

Millie consulted her guidebook. 'The first Senso-ji temple was erected on the site in 645 AD. But the whole place was bombed during the Second World War,' she read. 'Imagine if the original one was still here – it would be over a thousand years old.'

Jacinta pulled a face. 'You know, you don't have to tell us *every* detail about *every* place we visit.'

Millie poked out her tongue in return.

'Look at that!' Alice-Miranda pointed at a pretty pagoda to their left. It was five storeys high and looked like a tower of lacy cupcakes piled one on top of the other.

'It's gorgeous.' Millie ran closer and snapped some more photographs.

The group walked through the temple complex, admiring each of the buildings. Hugh was surprised when he glanced at his watch to realise that they had been there over two hours.

'So, Millie, what else is there for us to see close by?' Hugh asked.

'There's a market, just through there.' She pointed beyond the temple gate.

'Anyone want to join me for some shopping?' Hugh asked.

The girls nodded. Alice-Miranda was keen to buy gifts for everyone at home. She was on the lookout for a silk scarf for Shilly and something cute for Poppy and Jasper and Sloane, of course. And then there was Mr and Mrs Greening, Granny Bert, Daisy, Lily and Heinrich to think of too. And Max and Cyril.

'When will Aunt Charlotte and Uncle Lawrence and Lucas arrive?' Alice-Miranda asked her father. In all of the morning's excitement she'd almost forgotten they were coming.

'Your mother said they should be here tomorrow, providing Lawrence's movie has wrapped and they can get away,' Hugh replied.

'I can't wait until they arrive,' Jacinta sighed.

'No, you can't wait until your boyfriend arrives,' Millie teased.

'He's not my boyfriend,' Jacinta replied tersely. 'He's my future husband.'

'Does Lucas know that?' Millie asked.

'No, and I'll thank you not to tell him,' Jacinta retorted.

Alice-Miranda giggled as Jacinta and Millie pulled faces at one another. Even though the girls teased each other mercilessly at times, they had grown close over the past year.

The happy foursome wandered towards the shops. There were people everywhere perusing the narrow lane's market-style stores.

'Daddy, can we have a look on our own?' Alice-Miranda asked.

Hugh frowned. 'I don't want anyone getting lost.'

'But it's perfectly safe,' the child said. 'We'll just go in the same direction and meet you at the end of the row.'

The offer was tempting. Hugh had spotted a couple of antique shops and was keen to see if he could find an original suit of samurai armour. He thought one would look perfect in the corner of his study.

'All right, but stay together. I'll meet you at the gate down there with the bell, at say –' he glanced at his watch – 'one o'clock. Then we can go and find your mother and Ambrosia and have lunch.'

'Thanks, Daddy!' said Alice-Miranda, and she began to skip off.

'Do you need any money?' he called after her as the three girls disappeared into the crowd. 'Guess not.'

The trio wove their way through the masses and emerged in front of a shop selling lots of novelty items but mostly the same funny little creature. It had huge, round eyes and wore a cape and flying goggles, like a pilot from the olden days.

'I wonder what his name is,' Millie said as she inspected one of the porcelain figures.

A reed-thin man walked to the front of the shop

and bowed at the girls. His face was pockmarked and his thick black eyebrows furrowed fiercely.

'He is Itoshii Squirrel. It means Lovely Squirrel. He brings good luck.'

'Why does he wear that outfit?' Millie asked.

'He is a flying squirrel,' the man replied.

'Really?' Jacinta asked. 'Do Japanese squirrels *actually* fly?' The only Squirrels she'd ever seen scampered and scurried and were generally thought to be a nuisance.

'*Hai,*' he said. '*Momonga.*'

'*Momonga?*' Jacinta repeated.

'Well, I think Itoshii Squirrel is adorable.' Alice-Miranda walked further into the shop, browsing the apparently endless range of items dedicated to the tiny rodent. 'Poppy and Jasper will love him. Oh, and Sloane too.'

The man walked back behind the counter but his eyes followed the girls like a hawk. Jacinta watched him and wondered if he was always so suspicious of potential customers. Even grumpy Mr Munz in the village at Winchesterfield was more welcoming, and half the time he chased the children out of the shop – especially if his favourite television show, *Winners Are Grinners*, was about to come on.

Millie picked up a small pencil case and a matching set of coloured pencils. Alice-Miranda was keen on the figurines dressed in different superhero outfits for Jasper.

A plump boy entered the store. He stopped for a moment then continued to the counter, bumping into Jacinta on his way.

'*Sumimasen,*' he muttered but did not look at her.

'Yes, watch where you're going next time,' Jacinta huffed.

The man and the boy spoke in Japanese. Then the boy reached into his pocket and pulled out a bundle of bank notes, which he handed over. '*Yoku dekimashita!*' the man said with a laugh before the boy disappeared into the back of the shop.

Alice-Miranda and Millie finished their selections and walked to the counter. Millie had held onto the pencil case and pencils and added a mug, which she thought her mother might enjoy. Being a vet, she was always interested in animals – even if her patients tended not to wear capes.

Alice-Miranda deposited her small collection of items next to the cash register. She'd found a lovely set of coasters for Mrs Greening and a cute notepad for her husband, Harold.

The girls pulled out their wallets and paid for the goods.

The man leaned over and looked at Jacinta. 'What about in your pocket?'

Jacinta shook her head. 'There's nothing in my pocket.'

'You lie.'

'I do not,' she protested. 'I'll show you.' Jacinta fished around inside her jacket. She looked at the man and then at her friends, the colour draining from her cheeks.

'What's the matter?' Alice-Miranda asked.

Jacinta pulled out a small box. 'What's this?' She looked at it quizzically.

Alice-Miranda took it from her hand and opened it. Inside was a ring, with a crystal Itoshii Squirrel in the centre.

'You thief!' the man yelled. 'You steal the most expensive thing in my shop.'

'No, I didn't!' Jacinta's face was pale and she had begun to shake.

'I'm sure that it's just a misunderstanding,' Alice-Miranda said to the man. 'I'm happy to pay for it.'

He shook his head. 'No. No pay. I call the police.'

Through a sheer curtain in the back room, Millie could see the boy who had walked into the shop earlier. He was sitting at a small table looking up at a television set. There was a devilish smile on his lips.

'Please, I don't want to be in trouble.' Jacinta began to cry. 'I didn't do it. I promise. It must have fallen into my pocket.'

'Sir, I'm sure we can work this out,' Alice-Miranda said again.

In the distance, a conveniently timed siren wailed. 'You stay there. The police coming now,' said the shopkeeper.

Tears flooded Jacinta's face. 'But I didn't do anything,' she sobbed. Alice-Miranda put a comforting arm around her.

A sly grin settled on the man's face. 'Okay, I let you pay – double – and I won't get the police.'

Alice-Miranda looked at him in shock. 'Double! That's outrageous and I suspect it's illegal too.'

Millie was watching the scene playing out in front of her thinking that there had to be a perfectly rational explanation.

'Did that boy touch you?' she asked Jacinta. 'The one sitting through there?'

Jacinta stopped crying. She wiped her face and looked at Millie.

'Yes, he bumped into me when he walked into the shop,' Jacinta said.

'Well, that's it then.' Millie nodded decisively.

'That's what then?' Jacinta asked with a sniff.

'It was him. He put the box in your pocket.' Millie raised her eyebrows at the man, who suddenly seemed more interested in the ceiling than his customers.

'Are you sure?' Alice-Miranda asked. She knew Jacinta wasn't a thief but Millie's explanation was troubling. She marched around to the other side of the counter and through the curtain.

'Hey, what are you doing?' the man demanded. 'You can't go in there. Come back here.'

Upon seeing Alice-Miranda, the boy jumped from his chair and reeled backwards.

'*Sumimasen*,' said Alice-Miranda. She stared at the lad and held out the box. 'Do you think you might have accidentally dropped this into my friend's pocket?'

He looked at the item as if it was set to transform into a boy-eating beast at any second. His expression said it all. She'd caught him red-handed.

'I think you owe Jacinta an apology.' Alice-Miranda motioned at the girl, who was standing on the other side of the counter with her mouth open.

'Stupid!' The man rushed into the back room and gave the lad a sharp clip over the ear.

'Sir, there's absolutely no need for that.' Alice-Miranda leapt in front of the boy, who had begun to wail loudly.

'You mind your own business. This is between me and my son.' The man's eyes narrowed.

'I think setting up unsuspecting tourists is something the police would love to hear about,' Alice-Miranda said as she walked forward and dropped the box into the man's hand.

He looked at the child with her cascading chocolate curls and brown eyes as big as saucers as if wondering where she could possibly have come from. 'You are just a little girl. You don't scare me.'

'I wouldn't want to scare anyone,' Alice-Miranda said firmly. 'So Jacinta is free to go, isn't she?' She eyeballed the man, who said nothing, and then turned to her friends. 'Come on, girls.'

'It was just a joke. A silly trick. He didn't mean it,' the man called after them.

Alice-Miranda turned and shook her head. 'It wasn't very funny.'

The trio left the shop and stood outside. Jacinta's face was red and she was still shaking a little. 'Thank you,' she said. 'I can't believe he did that. What a little monster.'

'And the father was worse. Fancy trying to tell us it was a joke!' Millie glared towards the shop's door.

'It's just lucky you have excellent observation skills, Millie,' Alice-Miranda told her friend, then reached out and squeezed Jacinta's hand.

'We won't be going back there again,' Millie said. 'I don't care how cute Itoshii Squirrel is.'

Alice-Miranda glanced at her watch. 'Let's go and find Daddy.'

Chapter 9

Having served breakfast to the twenty elderly residents and washed up for the first time in her life, Kiko spent the next hour upstairs in the bedrooms rolling up futons and sweeping the *tatami*. She had expected to see yet more squirrels but the bedrooms were almost bare. The house was eerily quiet.

She tapped on the door at the far end of the hallway and slid it open.

'*Sumimasen!*' She bowed her head, surprised to see an old man sitting in a lounge chair. He was staring out the window and across the alley, with a leather-bound book perched on his knees.

Kiko looked at his bedding at the other end of the room and wondered what to do. 'May I tidy your room?' she asked quietly.

The man nodded.

Kiko rolled the futon and placed it into the cupboard as she had done in every other room. Then she retrieved the straw broom from the doorway and swept the matting. She was about to leave when the man spoke.

'You are new,' he said quietly.

'*Hai,*' she replied. She couldn't remember seeing the man at breakfast.

'Boy, haven't you finished yet?' Obaasan screeched from the bottom of the stairs. 'You are slower than those old people getting up and down the stairs, and that can take all day.' She cackled to herself. 'Time to do the washing.'

'She has a sharp tongue but a kind heart.'

Kiko realised that he was talking about Obaasan. '*Hai.*'

Kiko hesitated. She wanted to ask the old man if there was a way out of the house.

While she'd been cleaning, Kiko had investigated each room. Every window was deadlocked and there seemed to be very few external doors. Surely Obaasan would leave the house some time – and then Kiko would make her escape.

'You had better go, or her tongue will get sharper,' the old man said.

Kiko bowed and left the room.

In the hallway below, Kiko could hear shuffling and mumbling voices. A fresh smell replaced the fug that had clouded the dining room and Kiko realised that the residents had been bathing. She wondered why the old man upstairs had not gone down too, but then she remembered that his room seemed to be the only one with an ensuite.

Kiko scurried down the stairs and stopped in the doorway of the sitting room, where hundreds of squirrel figurines stared at her from every angle.

Obaasan was directing an old woman with wiry black hair to a seat. 'You sit there and I will get some tea.' Most of the chairs were occupied and several of the men and women were reading. Others were sleeping and some simply stared into space.

Obaasan walked over to her. 'There you are, boy.'

Without thinking, Kiko blurted the question she had been pondering all morning. 'Who *are* all these old people?'

'Aha! I knew you were not stupid. You do speak. They are my friends.'

'All of them are your friends?' Kiko frowned. She didn't know what it was like to have one friend, let alone twenty.

'*Hai!*' Obaasan curled her lip at Kiko. 'What? You think no one wants to be friends with an old lady like me. Bah! I am a spring lamb compared to that lot.'

Kiko found that hard to believe.

'They have no one to look after them, so I do it,' Obaasan continued. 'Some people collect *kokeshi* dolls or, even better, Itoshii Squirrel. I collect old people.'

'And Itoshii Squirrel,' Kiko said.

'I don't collect that silly rodent. I create him,' Obaasan said proudly.

Kiko was impressed.

'I know. I am sooo clever,' said Obaasan. 'And wait until you see what I have planned for him next.'

Kiko couldn't help thinking that, despite her gruffness and demands, Obaasan was very kind and generous to look after all of those people. And she was clever too: the squirrel was cute.

The old woman pulled a piece of paper from

her apron pocket and passed it to Kiko. 'What do you think?'

Kiko unfolded the page and had to stop herself from laughing out loud. It was a picture of a house with a giant flying squirrel on the roof.

'Or I could build him at the market.' The old woman reached out and turned the page over. Kiko recognised the bell gate, and beside it a giant squirrel was standing guard.

'Well, do you like it?' Obaasan asked.

Kiko nodded.

'It will be my special monument. But enough about squirrels. We're going to the laundry.' Obaasan shuffled along the hallway and stopped at a door beside the room Kiko had slept in. She pushed it open to reveal a small staircase leading to a basement. She pushed Kiko's shoulder. 'Off you go.'

'But what do I do?' the girl asked. She'd never done laundry in her life.

'You work it out. You're not as stupid as you look.'

Obaasan gave her a hefty shove and Kiko stumbled down the stairs. A bare globe cast dull yellow light around the room. A basket filled with clothes sat in one corner next to a rusty machine with a large stone tub beside it. A lone tear welled in the corner of Kiko's eye. She brushed it away and shook her head.

She'd known that running away would have consequences. That her life would change forever. But it was better than having to deal with her cruel aunt any longer, or a father who did not seem to care for her at all.

On the night before she left, Kiko had opened the cage door for her beloved canary, Mari. The little yellow bird had ventured to the entrance and hopped back inside the safety of her gilded home more than ten times before she flew to the window-sill. Down below, the garden beckoned and further away, the city seemed to spin around their oasis of calm. Mari sang a haunting song then turned once more to Kiko, before flying out into the world and disappearing forever. Kiko knew that the very next day she would do the same.

Now, the girl walked around the laundry room, looking for anything that might help her work out how she was to complete Obaasan's chore. A pair of scissors, a scrubbing brush and a large box of white powder sat on a long bench. Kiko peered at the writing and realised that this was soap for washing clothes. Then she turned her attention to the machine and read the faded characters around the dial.

She began to pull the clothing out of the basket and load it into the machine. When it seemed full, she fiddled with the controls and was surprised and pleased when water began to pour in. She added a large scoop of powder and then another two for good measure. She watched the machine like a hawk, jumping every time it clanged and banged.

After a little while, Kiko noticed froth escaping from around the lid. She didn't want to touch the contraption while it was in motion but the bubbles began to run down the front of it and onto the floor. Kiko froze. The bubbles were multiplying and the space around her was filling fast. She could barely see the machine any more and had swallowed a few bubbles too, which were burning her throat.

The door at the top of the stairs opened and Obaasan screeched, 'Are you finished down there?'

Kiko scurried to the stairs and called back, 'Soon.' She hoped that the old woman couldn't see in the dim light – although she wasn't sure Obaasan could see much at all, especially without her glasses.

'What are you doing? Not washing by hand, I hope. That's why I have a super-fast, modern machine – at least it was when I bought it thirty years ago,' Obaasan cackled. 'Are you really going to make an old woman come down there?'

'No!' Kiko called back. 'I just spilled some water.' Around her the bubbles that had threatened to engulf the whole room were fizzling away.

'Then come up here. You are lazy. I have more jobs for you to do,' the old woman shouted.

'I'm coming.' Kiko ran up the rickety staircase and into the hall.

'Did you separate the washing?' Obaasan asked.

The girl gulped. She didn't know that she was supposed to do that. She wondered how she would separate it anyway – into what?

'Idiot boy.' Obaasan shook her head. 'If everything comes out pink you will not be popular.'

Pink? Kiko had no idea how she could possibly turn all of the clothes pink. That sounded like magic and she knew after years of trying to cast a disappearing spell on her aunt that she had no such powers.

'You hang it up to dry?' Obaasan asked.

'The machine was still going,' Kiko stammered.

'Go back later – don't forget or Ojiisan will not be happy. He has a cane and he does not mind using it.' Obaasan pulled a face that made her look even more like a dried prune than usual.

Kiko wondered which Ojiisan she was referring to. There were many grandfathers in the house and Kiko did not want to encounter any of their canes.

'Come, I have a new job for you.' Obaasan shuffled along the hall and into the kitchen. Kiko followed and was surprised to find a plump boy sitting at the kitchen table.

'Hey, fat boy, this is Yoshi.' Obaasan pointed at Kiko. 'Fat boy is Taro. He has the right name, don't you think?' Obaasan scoffed.

Kiko shrugged, wondering what she meant.

'Taro – it means eldest son who is fat. I know, I am so funny!' the old woman hooted.

Kiko kept her eyes low and tried not to look at the boy. Fortunately he was too busy shovelling food into his mouth to be interested in the new arrival. Kiko glanced from the boy's bowl to the huge pot of noodles boiling on the stove. It must be close to lunchtime, she realised.

Obaasan motioned for Kiko to sit at the table. A tall stack of letters bound by an elastic band leaned precariously next to the boy called Taro. 'Your next job.'

Kiko was surprised. She had expected to be serving noodles again.

'You open these for me and sort into piles,' the woman said. 'One pile is for payments for the old people, the other is for bills. Tick them off against the names here.'

Taro looked up. 'But that's my job.' A dribble of liquid ran down his chin and he sucked a noodle through his teeth. It disappeared like a beach worm into the sand.

'I am trying someone new,' the old woman said. 'You are too slow and too stupid.'

Kiko sat on the chair opposite the hungry lad and looked at the mound of mail. She'd never opened a letter in her life. There seemed to be a lot of names on the list. Kiko had only counted twenty residents plus the man she had found upstairs earlier in the morning. She wondered if Obaasan had another house full of old people somewhere else.

The old woman shuffled over to the bench and returned with a long, sharp object. Kiko flinched. Obaasan pulled the first letter from the pile and slashed it open. Kiko breathed again.

'You put money coming in here.' She slapped her hand on the table. 'And bills go here.' She pounded her palm on the opposite side. 'And don't mix them up. My son says that fat boy is always wrong.'

Kiko unfolded the first letter. She scanned the page, reading it as quickly as she could. At the bottom was an amount and it looked like the person named at the top was to receive this money. She placed it to her left, then opened the second envelope and repeated the action. Soon there was a stack of papers to her left and just a couple to her right. The payment statements were all from the government and when Kiko mentally added them together, it seemed like a very large sum of money.

Obaasan stopped stirring the pot on the stove and nodded. 'You are good at sorting.'

Taro looked up just as Kiko did. He stuck his tongue out at her and pulled a monster face.

Kiko couldn't help it. She laughed. It only made Taro madder.

'Give me that.' Taro snatched the last page from Kiko's hand and looked at it. He added it to the payment pile.

Kiko shook her head. As she picked it up and moved it to the other side, her eyes came to rest on what she thought was a date of birth. Kiko pondered for a moment before realising just how long ago it was. She studied the form and wondered who it belonged to.

'Obaasan, how old is the oldest person in the house?' Kiko asked quietly.

'Mmm, one of the Ojiisans is turning one hundred and two next birthday. He is old enough to be *my* grandfather.'

Kiko glanced up at her. She didn't think that could be true. Kiko looked at the birth date on the page. This person would be turning one hundred and fourteen.

'Is his name Sato-san?'

Obaasan wrinkled her nose. 'Sato-san went years ago.'

A man with a pockmarked face walked through the kitchen door. He looked at Kiko and the papers beside her, then strode over and snatched up the pile. He walked back to the stove where Obaasan was standing. 'What is he doing?' he hissed at the woman.

'Sorting,' Obaasan replied.

'Are you stupid?' the man snapped.

'Watch your tongue, my son. This boy is smart and you said yourself that Taro makes too many mistakes.'

'This boy is not family. How do we know we can trust him?' the man demanded.

Kiko kept her head down but stole glances in their direction. The man walked back to the table and sat down heavily. 'Who are you, boy?'

Kiko gulped. 'Yoshi,' she whispered.

'What did you see here?' He pointed at the pages.

Kiko shook her head. 'Nothing.'

'That's right. You saw nothing. Our business is our business and you will do well to keep your nose out of it.'

Kiko nodded and kept her mouth closed.

Taro smirked at her.

Obaasan shuffled over from the stove and stood beside the man. 'What are you talking about, Tatsu? We have nothing to hide!'

'But this boy does. Why are you wearing your hat inside?' the man asked, staring at Kiko.

Obaasan hadn't said anything about her cap.

'Take it off so I can see you,' the man demanded.

Kiko flinched. 'I have to finish the washing.' She stood and fled from the room, racing down the corridor and into the laundry below.

She didn't like the man in the kitchen, but whatever he was doing was none of her business. She had her own troubles. Kiko's hand trembled as she picked up the large pair of scissors she'd noticed earlier.

Chapter 10

Dolly Oliver fluffed her trademark brown curls, powdered her nose and smacked her rose-coloured lips together. Dressed in her favourite navy suit and cream blouse, she felt as if she was on top of the world – which could have had something to do with the stunning view from her generously proportioned room on the forty-fifth floor of the hotel.

She couldn't remember the last time she'd slept so well, which was remarkable, as she'd gone to bed feeling anxious about her impending presentation.

It was scheduled for the following afternoon but her speech still needed tweaking.

Dolly sat down at the desk under the windows, and looked at the vast city below. Somewhere, Alice-Miranda and her friends would be out exploring, she thought to herself with a smile. Dolly was looking forward to joining them once the conference was finished later in the week.

She opened her folder and read through her speech again, marking changes as she went.

Although Dolly's formal training had been limited, after some experimentation she discovered that she had something of a gift for science. It was fortunate that her first employers, Cecelia's parents, had recognised Dolly's potential early on and were pleased to support her scientific endeavours. Plus, they had thought Dolly to be the best cook in the world, so if letting her potter with her inventions meant that she would remain in their employ forever, the Highton-Smiths had been more than happy for her to do so.

Dolly now had a splendid laboratory in the cellars at Highton Hall.

The creation of Just Add Water, or JAW as it was more commonly known, had been a labour of love over many years after the tragic death of her husband. An explorer of great renown, Dougal Oliver had perished during a blizzard when he had run out of food. Dolly had thought that a light-weight, compact product that transformed into nutritious food would not only benefit those under-taking outdoor pursuits but could also help reduce world hunger. And she had been right.

Hugh Kennington-Jones was so impressed with the product's potential that he had immediately had a manufacturing plant built adjacent to the Kennington's supermarket headquarters.

And now with JAW contracts signed in more than twenty-eight countries, the invention was being rolled out around the globe.

Dolly smiled to herself. She couldn't believe that her years of dabbling had brought her all the way to Japan to speak in front of eminent scientists from all over the world. She finished reading through her notes and turned her attention to the small pill case at the side of the desk. She opened it to reveal three compartments of white pills. Each group bore its own stamp: a rising sun, the Eiffel Tower and a bull. She'd been pleased with her whimsical thinking, and it would be impossible to get them mixed up.

Dolly decided that she should take one before she made her way down to breakfast. At home she'd run several trials, but only when she was alone in the laboratory practising her language skills. The pills had worked almost perfectly but there was still room for improvement. Even she found it hard to explain the science behind her new invention, but it had the potential to change lives if she could get it right.

She stood up and took a small bottle of water from the bar fridge beside the desk. 'Let's see how this goes,' she said and swallowed one of the pills marked with a rising sun.

★

An hour later, the young girl at the entrance to the hotel restaurant smiled and bowed at the old woman with the perfectly coiffed curls.

'Good morning, Mrs Oliver,' she said with a nod.

Dolly read the girl's name tag and said, in Japanese, 'Good morning, Umi-san. What a pleasant morning it is.'

The girl looked a little startled, and then smiled and replied in Japanese, 'Yes, it is. May I compliment your command of Japanese. It is perfect, ma'am, unlike my attempts at English.'

'I'm sure we'll all find it much easier to speak one another's native tongues one of these days,' Dolly replied. She smiled and bowed. Oh, how pleased she was with the first test!

'This way.' The girl held out her arm and asked Mrs Oliver to follow her.

Chapter 11

Alice-Miranda reached out to hold Jacinta's hand. 'Are you all right?'

'Yes, it was just a bit of a shock. I mean, seriously, I could have given that little tub of lard a run for his money if I'd wanted to. But I had no idea what he and his father were saying to one another or if they were serious about calling the police. I don't think I'd like to go to prison in a foreign country.'

'As opposed to going to prison at home?' Millie said. 'I can see how that would be *so* much nicer.'

Jacinta sighed. 'You know what I mean.'

Millie gave Jacinta a grin and patted her on the shoulder.

'Hello Daddy,' called Alice-Miranda as she spotted her father coming out of a store near the end of the row.

Hugh swivelled around to face the girls. 'Hello darling, did you have any luck with your shopping?'

Alice-Miranda nodded and held up her bags. 'I got some lovely presents and so did Millie.'

'What about you, Jacinta?' Hugh asked. He noticed that her eyes were red and she didn't look her usual perky self.

'There was a bit of trouble,' Millie piped up. 'The owner of the shop accused Jacinta of stealing.'

'He did what!'

'It's all right, Daddy. It was just a misunderstanding and we sorted it out,' Alice-Miranda explained.

'Alice-Miranda sorted him out, that's for sure.' Millie shot an admiring look at her friend.

Hugh listened to the girls' tale. He was keen to go back and give the man and the boy a piece of his mind, but Alice-Miranda said that there was nothing to gain. At least the boy had been caught red-handed.

'I don't think that's quite the point,' Hugh said. 'I've heard about things like this happening in tourist areas.'

'I think they were trying to be clever,' Alice-Miranda said. 'And the father did apologise and said that they were just having a bit of a joke.'

'It wasn't funny,' Millie said.

Jacinta pouted and nodded.

Hugh reluctantly agreed not to pursue the matter. He didn't want to get into a row and it sounded as if Alice-Miranda had handled herself perfectly.

Hugh glanced at his watch. It was after one. 'Well, what about some lunch? Cecelia and Ambrosia have been caught up and won't be able to join us, so they said they'd meet us in the city about half past two. What are we going to eat? There are plenty of restaurants along here.' Hugh looked at the row of shops. 'I spotted some tasty-looking eels and a couple of blowfish in one of the live tanks.'

Jacinta and Millie pulled faces at one another.

Hugh grinned mischievously.

'Daddy, please stop teasing. What about teppan-yaki?' Alice-Miranda asked. 'I feel like some beef.'

Jacinta immediately perked up. 'Oh, yes please.'

'I'm happy with that,' Millie agreed.

Hugh led the girls to a restaurant he'd noticed earlier. They entered and were instantly surrounded by the tantalising smell of sizzling beef. A smiling chef in a crisp white uniform greeted the group with a bow as they took their seats around a giant barbecue plate in the centre of the room. The chef sliced some perfectly cooked meat at lightning speed and served three plates to some patrons on the other side of the counter.

'Are you happy for me to order?' Hugh asked. 'I was thinking some chicken and beef.'

The girls agreed.

'Unless of course you'd like to try the blowfish?'

Millie and Jacinta screwed up their noses.

Alice-Miranda laughed. 'I think that's definitely a no.'

Hugh placed the order then chatted with the girls about their purchases.

'Did you buy anything, Daddy?' Alice-Miranda asked.

'Yes, but don't tell your mother,' he said and winked.

Her eyes lit up. 'Is it a present?'

'No, but I'm sure she'll get a surprise when she sees it in my study.' Hugh couldn't hide his grin as he told the girls about his find: a handsomely preserved suit of sixteenth-century samurai armour, which he had arranged to have shipped home.

'Poor Shilly, can you imagine her shock when she opens it?' Alice-Miranda giggled.

'No worse than when I found that antique taxi-dermy polar bear in the cellar and had it brought up until we could find it a new home at the museum,' her father replied.

'I remember that. It was horrible. Poor creature. I'm sure that Great-Grandpa Highton only had him in the house because it was fashionable. I'm glad that these days sensible people prefer to admire animals in their natural habitat rather than shooting them and putting them in the sitting room.'

'Yes, darling, I couldn't agree more,' her father nodded. 'Now, I did buy some other bits and pieces and I was going to keep them until later, but . . .'

'But you're hopeless at keeping secrets,' Alice-Miranda chimed in.

'You know me far too well.' Hugh hung his head in mock shame. Then he reached down and produced a dainty bag from which he pulled three exquisitely wrapped boxes. They were covered in the most beautiful shiny paper with scenes of cherry blossoms and castles, and tied with perfect gold bows.

'One for you.' Hugh passed Jacinta a box. 'And one for you.' He reached across and gave Millie another. 'And this is for you, sweetheart.' He dropped a third box into Alice-Miranda's hand and planted a kiss on the top of her head.

'Daddy, you didn't have to buy us presents,' said Alice-Miranda.

'I know, but when I saw these I thought they'd be the perfect memento of our trip – and I knew your mother would love them too,' Hugh said.

The girls each examined their gifts.

'I'm dying to know what's inside,' said Jacinta. She studied the box closely then gave it a shake next to her ear.

'I don't want to touch it,' Millie said. 'I've never seen anything so perfectly presented. My gifts always look like they were wrapped by a spider wearing boxing gloves – I can never get the paper straight when I cut it and I always end up using half the sticky tape roll to keep it together.'

'Go on, girls, I want you to open them,' said Hugh with a sparkle in his eyes. 'What do you say we take a photograph and then you can dive in.'

Millie pulled her camera from her blue backpack and lined the trio of boxes up on the counter in front of them. She snapped away, then Hugh took some pictures of the girls holding them and finally a waitress offered to take another couple of shots of Hugh and the girls together.

After they'd covered just about every photographic scenario, all three girls began to unwrap their presents.

'Turn the other way,' Millie said, 'so we can't see what each other got until we've all unwrapped them. But Alice-Miranda, don't take forever or we'll show you.'

'Aha! You're assuming that you've all got the same,' Hugh said.

'Are they different?' Alice-Miranda asked.

'You'll just have to hurry up and see.'

Jacinta was first to gasp. 'Oh my goodness, it's lovely!' She beamed at Hugh while carefully concealing her treasure.

Millie was just as enthusiastic. 'It's beautiful. Is it real gold?'

'Daddy!' Alice-Miranda's voice dropped. 'You'll have to take mine back.'

Millie and Jacinta wondered why she sounded so

disappointed. Hugh frowned. There was an awkward silence.

'I'm kidding! It's gorgeous.' Alice-Miranda turned back to her father and gave him a tight squeeze.

'Oh, you little monster,' Hugh sighed.

The girls helped one another put their gifts on before properly examining each necklace.

Jacinta was wearing a pretty gold chain with a dainty charm in the shape of a paper crane.

'It's lovely,' said Millie and Alice-Miranda as they admired the intricate detail.

Millie's charm was a tiny gold branch of cherry blossoms, while Alice-Miranda wore a small circular pendant.

'What is that?' Jacinta asked.

'It's a chrysanthemum,' Hugh replied. 'It's a symbol of the Japanese royal family. The Emperor sits on the Chrysanthemum throne.'

'Ooh, uncomfortable,' Jacinta said, squirming in her seat.

Millie shook her head. 'You're ridiculous.'

'What?' Jacinta said, grinning. 'Chrysanthemums are spiky. And I'm not ridiculous, thank you very much.'

'Maybe, maybe not,' Millie said and then turned

to Hugh. 'Thanks, Hugh.' She slid down from her seat and gave him a hug. Jacinta did the same, followed by Alice-Miranda.

'So, I did okay?' he asked.

'Yes, Daddy – perfect!' Alice-Miranda smiled as she admired her pendant. 'I'm going to wear it every day. Well, at least until we go back to school. Miss Grimm isn't fond of jewellery with our uniforms.'

Millie and Jacinta agreed that they would do the same.

Chapter 12

Kiko listened at the top of the basement stairs. She had stayed in the laundry as long as she dared. At least the clothes were clean and, as far as she could tell in the poor light, not pink. She'd hung everything on the taut cables that spanned the room, hoping that was how the laundry was normally dried. She didn't mind having to do the jobs at all — in fact, she was quite enjoying doing something for others instead of studying from dawn to dusk. But she had to uncover a way out and ask for help to find the house she was seeking. She couldn't stay with Obaasan and her squirrels forever.

Kiko pulled her cap lower and went to tuck her hair back inside. She felt for her plait but of course it was no longer there. It was hidden inside her t-shirt. She had thought it would be more difficult – her hair had always been long – but in a couple of sharp chops it was done. She'd tidied it up as best she could and wondered what she looked like now. It was strange; she felt so much lighter.

The house was silent. Kiko tiptoed along the hallway to her room. Once inside, she found her backpack, opened the zip and stuffed the plait in. She wondered if she might be able to sell it. Surely there were wigmakers who would pay for good quality hair. Kiko pulled out her jacket. She dug her hand into the pocket and froze. Her fingers searched every corner – then the other pocket too. But nothing.

She up-ended the bag, wondering if it had fallen out when she'd put her jacket inside the previous evening. The diary fell to the floor and her plait tumbled on top of it but nothing else. She unzipped the front pouch. It was empty too. Kiko shook the futon, hoping desperately that her necklace had slipped out and fallen among the bedding.

'Are you in there, boy?' Obaasan called from somewhere down the hall.

Kiko hurriedly fixed her bed and stuffed her jacket and hair inside the backpack. She placed the diary carefully down the side and zipped the bag up. Her heart beat even faster than when she'd been caught at the turnstile in the subway. She gasped for breath.

That boy – Taro – he must have been snooping in her room. He could have taken it, or his father, Tatsu. Kiko had felt the necklace in her pocket before she'd dozed off outside the door last night. It was right there and now it was gone. What if it had fallen out while she was sleeping on the doorstep? Kiko couldn't think.

She wanted to get out of the house. Her head was spinning. She ran to the hallway and looked towards the back door – but the padlocks were still in place.

'Yoshi, you come here now,' Obaasan yelled.

Kiko turned and saw the old woman shuffling towards her. She felt as if she might throw up.

'What are you staring at the door for? Never mind those locks. They are to keep the old people in. I can't have them wandering off. Are you hungry, boy?'

Kiko's stomach was in knots. Food was the last thing she felt like.

'I called you for lunch but you were still doing the laundry. Did you do the ironing too?' Obaasan asked. 'If that's the case, I will keep you forever.'

The clothes weren't even dry and Kiko hadn't the first clue about ironing.

'Well, I have left you some noodles and chicken and rice,' Obaasan said. 'You did a good job with the sorting. Better than fat boy. He is my grandson and the stupidest boy I have ever known. Maybe I will get rid of him and keep you instead.'

'Does Taro do other jobs?' Kiko asked quietly. She was hoping he had some chores outside the house.

'What did you say, boy? Speak up! My hearing is not as good since my last birthday. Eighty-two and suddenly you are on the downhill slide, though I am still a baby compared with that lot in there.' Obaasan pointed her thumb over her shoulder towards the sitting room.

'I could go to the market for you,' Kiko said a little louder. Kiko had seen grocery bags in the kitchen the day before and wondered who was responsible for the shopping.

'Mmm. Taro is always messing up my order. If you like, you can go to the market tomorrow. I have a very looooong list.'

'Do you need me to go today?' Kiko asked. She was desperate to get outside and search the alley for her necklace.

Obaasan shook her head. 'No.'

The old woman shuffled past Kiko into the bedroom.

She reached under the covers and pulled out Kiko's backpack.

'I will look after this for you.'

Kiko's heart froze. 'Why?' she whispered.

'This is my insurance. I don't want you to take my shopping money and run off, boy.' Obaasan grinned. Flecks of noodles sat between her yellow teeth. 'Whatever is in this bag must be important to you. I'm sure you would have run away last night if it hadn't been sitting under my foot. I will give it back once I am sure I can trust you.' The old woman unzipped the top and pulled out the change of clothes Kiko had brought with her. 'But you can keep these. I don't want you to smell bad.' Obaasan held them out. She squinted through her glasses. 'Mmm . . . maybe you are not so good at washing – have you turned your own underpants pink?'

Kiko quickly snatched the underpants and white t-shirt. She felt sick. Her necklace was already gone. There was no way she could lose her mother's diary too.

Chapter 13

Hatsuko stared at the screen. A bald man beside her was fiddling with a piece of electronic equipment on the desk. Her two black-suited assistants stood watching too. A map of Tokyo appeared and within a few seconds the image zoomed in on a red blip. It was moving along a street in the area called Asakusa.

'Aha!' Hatsuko exclaimed. 'Am I not a genius?' The woman leaned closer to the screen. 'But what is she doing there?'

Yuki and Yamato shrugged.

Hatsuko turned to the technician. 'How quickly will the car be ready?'

'It will take another day,' he replied, his eyes downcast.

'Work faster. I need her to be in the safe house as soon as possible,' Hatsuko hissed.

'I could take another car,' Yuki suggested. 'And Yamato could guide me from here.'

Hatsuko thought for a moment then shook her head. 'You cannot take her off the street in broad daylight. Anyway, I'm sure it is just a coincidence she is in that part of the city. She won't find what she's looking for.'

'But isn't it dangerous for her to be outside? What if someone realises?' said Yamato.

'Perhaps you should have thought of that before you lost her! She has run away, numbskull. She doesn't want to be found. She will be lying low and realising just how hard life can be. But I'm certain that the last thing she wants is to come back here,' Hatsuko said, arching an eyebrow.

The men nodded.

'So, today you will track her every movement on this screen and make note of the places that she goes,' said Hatsuko. 'And I don't need to remind you what will happen if you fail a second time.'

They gulped and chorused, 'No.'

Hatsuko stood and stalked out of the room. She climbed the narrow stairwell to the ground floor and locked the small door behind her. A man's voice startled her. 'Good morning, Hatsuko. What are you doing down here?'

Hatsuko swivelled around and bowed at Kenzo. Her mind raced. She'd never run into him here before. 'Exercise,' she replied. 'It is good to walk the long way around some days. And you?'

'My intentions are far less noble. I've come to see if there is any *daifuku* for my morning tea.'

'There is a telephone to the kitchen,' she said, 'and plenty of eager young women to bring the cake to you.'

'Of course, but if I at least have to walk here, I don't feel quite so guilty about my greedy belly.'

Hatsuko nodded curtly and bowed. 'I must go.' She turned to walk away.

'I think there will be good news today,' Kenzo said.

Hatsuko stopped in her tracks. 'What good news?' A tingle of excitement surged through her body. She hoped it was the news she had been waiting for.

'Please walk with me and I will explain.' Kenzo and Hatsuko headed down the long passageway. 'Tomorrow the motion that will ensure the family's future will go before the parliament,' he said, glancing over at her.

A smile crept onto Hatsuko's face.

'I see you are pleased.'

'Oh yes, this is perfect,' she said, nodding. 'It has been a long time coming.'

'I am so glad that you approve.' Kenzo smiled.

'This will change everything.'

'It will be a blessing for us all,' said Kenzo. 'Kiko should know that her position is secure, but perhaps don't mention anything to her just yet. Is she feeling better?'

Hatsuko flinched at the mention of the child. 'No, she is still poorly. And I must go check on her.'

Kenzo bowed and Hatsuko hurried along, her heart fit to burst. Soon. She had waited so long and now it seemed that her patience would finally be rewarded.

Chapter 14

After a delicious lunch, Hugh and the girls were set to meet Cecelia and Ambrosia in an area called Harajuku, which was famous for attracting young people who loved fashion and manga cartoons. Ambrosia had been interviewing several of the young fashionistas there and one of the designers had offered to take the children on a tour to see the young men and women dressed in their outrageous costumes. When Ambrosia had called earlier to say she couldn't make lunch, she'd arranged with Hugh to bring the girls over to meet her and Cecelia. The Meiji Shrine was also close by and Hugh thought they might have time to visit there too.

'I think we'll pop back to the *ryokan* and you girls can drop off your shopping first,' Hugh said as the girls tripped along beside him. 'Then I'll order a car.'

'Really, Daddy? A car? That's not very adventurous,' said Alice-Miranda.

'What do you suggest?' Jacinta asked her. 'A flying saucer?'

Alice-Miranda smiled. 'Ha ha. I was thinking that we should try the subway.'

'Oh, I'm not sure about that,' said Hugh, flinching. 'I've never used it before and none of us speak Japanese.'

'It can't be that hard, Daddy. I've been on the subway in New York and the three of us have been on the Paris Metro, and it's a great way to get around,' Alice-Miranda said. 'It helps you see the real city — and you said that's why we were staying in the *ryokan* and not a hotel.'

'I'm up for it,' said Millie.

'Me too,' Jacinta agreed.

'Looks like I'm outvoted. But I'm going to get some directions from Aki first.' Hugh pushed open the door to the inn and the girls walked into the front foyer, where they quickly exchanged their shoes for slippers.

Aki was standing behind the reception desk.

'*Konnichiwa,*' she said, bowing.

'*Konnichiwa,*' the girls chorused back.

'Why don't you run along upstairs and put your things away, girls. I'll see if Aki can help me with a map,' Hugh suggested.

The girls waved to the young woman and scurried away down the hall.

★

The train pulled into the station and Alice-Miranda's group alighted. Hugh consulted the map Aki had marked up for him and led the children towards one of the exits. He was looking for Takeshita Street, where they were to meet Cecelia and Ambrosia and their guide.

'Isn't the station lovely?' Alice-Miranda turned and pointed at the gabled roof and the little turret on top. A large clock sat above the entrance.

'It looks like something from Tudor times,' Millie said. 'Mixed in with modern day.'

Groups of teenagers dressed like life-sized dolls and superheroes stood in groups talking and posing for photographs around the station entrance. Alice-Miranda stopped to say hello to two girls in rainbow dresses with matching pink hair and sparkling eye make-up. Millie asked if she could take a photograph and the girls nodded enthusiastically. Hugh offered to take the picture, so the girls could get in together. Alice-Miranda, Millie and Jacinta stood between the Japanese girls, who held their fingers out in 'V' peace signs.

'Smile,' Hugh said as he pressed the button.

'*Arigatou,*' Alice-Miranda called, as the older girls bowed and walked away. She turned to her friends. 'They look amazing, don't they? Oh, look, there's Mummy!' She'd spotted her mother and Ambrosia in the crowd ahead.

Hugh led the girls up the busy street. Ambrosia introduced them to a young woman called Michiko, who was wearing long pink socks and a short dress that looked like a cross between Cinderella's gown and a school uniform.

'I've never seen so much pink,' Millie whispered. 'Do you think Barbie lives around here somewhere?'

Alice-Miranda grinned. It certainly looked that

way. She half-expected to see a pink campervan drive around the corner at any minute.

Michiko explained how the neighbourhood's association with inventive clothing started. 'Japanese teenagers are mad for manga. Some began dressing like their favourite characters and it grew from there. Now Harajuku is famous all over the world for the weird and wacky fashions we wear.'

'Does it take long to get ready in the morning?' Millie asked. She couldn't think of anything worse than spending hours at a time working out what to wear.

'Quite a long time. Is anyone hungry?' Michiko asked.

Millie and Jacinta nodded.

'That's good, because we have a great crepe restaurant just along here. I thought we would have a snack before I take you to the store.'

'Crepes? In Japan?' Millie said. 'I loved the crepes in Paris. I wonder if these are the same – they don't have any strange sea creatures in them, do they?'

'No.' Michiko shook her head and smiled. 'No sea creatures at all. Just chocolate.'

Millie rubbed her tummy. 'That sounds good to me!'

Chapter 15

Dolly Oliver had enjoyed a leisurely morning wandering through the bustling streets around her hotel. Shinjuku was a vibrant part of the city, with enormous electronic billboards on every corner and stores selling everything from computers to silk fans and kitsch novelties. It wasn't often that Dolly was on her own. Even when her employers were away, Shilly was always about and Millie's grandfather, Ambrose, spent a lot of time with her these days too. She rather wished he'd been able to join her on the trip, but he was in the process of selling up his farm and had to oversee the livestock sale. He had recently bought himself a delightful cottage in Highton Mill on the edge of the Highton-Smith-Kennington-Jones estate. He told people that it was so he could be closer to facilities in case of an emergency but everyone knew that it had more to do with Dolly than any doctor.

Dolly had taken great delight in speaking to the shopkeepers in Japanese. She'd chatted away easily as she bought gifts, including a pretty wooden *kokeshi* doll for Alice-Miranda and a silk purse for Shilly. By her calculations the effect of the tablet was due to wear off at any minute. The opening speech for the conference would commence at two o'clock, giving Dolly enough time to take her parcels back to her room.

In the auditorium foyer, Dolly scanned the growing crowd. She didn't recognise anyone and she was beginning to feel a little intimidated. A tall Japanese man walked towards her and bowed.

'Good afternoon, Mrs Oliver, it is very pleasing to make your acquaintance,' the man said. 'I am Nobu Taguchi from the Japanese Ministry for Invention and Innovation.'

Dolly smiled at the young man and extended her hand. He was the one who had telephoned her last week. She thought him very handsome. He was tall and muscular, and reminded her a little of Lawrence Ridley.

As she began to speak, she answered his question in perfect Japanese – except that on this occasion she hadn't meant to. She wanted to speak to him in English as he had done with her.

Nobu smiled broadly and complimented her excellent language skills.

Dolly gulped. Something was wrong. She could think in English but she couldn't speak it.

'We are blessed to have many participants from around the world – but I must warn you, Mrs Oliver, that not many will be as skilled in the use of the Japanese language as you,' said Nobu as he guided her towards a group of delegates.

Dolly undid the buttons on her blazer and fanned herself with the program as Nobu interrupted the huddle and brought one of the men out to meet her. She began to wonder if the air-conditioning was working properly.

'Professor Dimble, may I introduce Mrs Oliver, the inventor of JAW,' said Nobu. He extended his arm towards a portly gentleman whose eyebrows resembled a pair of fuzzy caterpillars. The man wore a yellow waistcoat with a matching cravat and a pair of round glasses perched on the very tip of his nose.

'Oh, yes.' The professor looked at Dolly and nodded. From the tone of his voice and the slight curl of his lip, Dolly didn't think he was especially pleased to meet her.

She smiled back and bowed slightly, not game to open her mouth.

'Now tell me, Mrs Oliver, – it is *Mrs* Oliver, not Doctor or Professor, isn't it?' he said with a sneer. 'What on earth possessed you to use baked dinners? That's a very pedestrian meal, don't you think?'

Dolly looked at the man. She pressed her lips together in an awkward smile.

'Mrs Oliver, are you all right?' Nobu prompted. He thought perhaps the woman was a little hard of hearing.

'Mmm,' she nodded.

'What's the matter, Mrs Oliver? Cat got your tongue?' the professor asked. He wondered if the woman was as stupid as she looked.

Inside, Dolly was seething. She couldn't help herself. She launched into a detailed response to the professor's initial question – except that it was in perfect Japanese. 'In our family a baked dinner has always been the ultimate comfort food and I could think of no better place to start – of course you do know that we've expanded into other meals including curries and stews to better suit the markets we've entered.'

Nobu gave her a quizzical look. Professor Dimble looked as though he had just sucked a very large lemon.

Dolly asked if her Japanese friend would translate what she had said. Nobu frowned and nodded, then explained to the Professor.

'I see,' Professor Dimble said with a smirk. 'I don't suppose Mrs Oliver could have just told me that herself. Then again, I'd probably feel a little out of my depth here too, with all these *real* academics.'

Beads of perspiration began to trickle from Dolly's temples and she could feel the heat rising in her neck. Professor Dimble was the rudest person she'd met in a very long time. Who did he think he was, questioning her qualifications, making her feel as if she didn't deserve to be there? She wondered what his contribution to the world of science had been.

Nobu could see her agitation. 'Would you like me to get you a glass of water, Mrs Oliver?'

Dolly politely declined and excused herself, walking at top speed towards the powder room.

Apart from feeling as though she could strangle Professor Dimble, she was worried about the tablet. She'd never had this problem before. Although she was thinking in English, no matter how hard she tried, it was Japanese that formed on her lips.

She looked at her watch. In the past, the effects of the tablet had worn off in about four hours. But that was before she fiddled with the formula again last week. She'd taken the tablet at half past seven and it was now almost two. Something had gone terribly wrong and Dolly hadn't a clue how to fix it. She'd been working on a neutraliser to take in the event of such an emergency, but it was still in the laboratory at home, waiting to be perfected.

The powder room was a large and extravagant affair with a chaise longue in the corner of the entrance vestibule. She'd just have to sit it out — at least until the delegates entered the auditorium and she could scamper to the lifts and back up to her room.

Chapter 16

In their basement den, Yuki and Yamato hadn't taken their eyes off the screen for over an hour. They'd stared intently as the pulsing red dot wound through the streets of Asakusa. Then suddenly it had disappeared. They'd stared at the screen as if by willpower alone they could bring the dot back to life.

'Where did it go?' Yamato groaned. He'd leaned forward, his nose almost touching the monitor.

Yuki had anxiously phoned the technician who'd set up the display.

'Mmm, I thought this could happen. That tracker has always been faulty,' the man had said.

'Does Hatsuko know this?' Yuki asked.

The man sniffed loudly. 'No. This technology hasn't been tested for years and I forgot it was even there. She'd forgotten too until you mentioned the necklace. I fitted it years ago to keep track of the girl and make sure that she was safe. But now we know better . . . I'll come by when I'm finished with the car.' And with that he'd hung up, leaving Yuki and Yamato staring at the blank screen.

The blip had sprung back to life a while later. It was now a long way from Asakusa. The men were surprised to see it heading towards them and wondered if Kiko had changed her mind about running away.

The two of them were concentrating so intently they didn't hear Hatsuko enter the room.

'What do you see?' she demanded, leaning in between them.

The two men almost leapt through the roof.

'*Sumimasen,*' they said as they composed themselves.

'Kiko has travelled this afternoon. She is not far from here,' said the taller man, Yuki, as he pointed at the dot on the screen.

He had his other hand on his lap, crossing his fingers that the blip stayed alive while Hatsuko was present.

'I see,' she said, peering closer. 'So why hasn't one of you gone to find her?'

'You told us not to,' Yuki gulped.

Hatsuko glared at the men and shook her head. 'That was when she was miles away. She is too close to home now.'

Yamato looked at his partner. 'I will go,' he said, without moving from his seat.

'Well, what are you waiting for?' Hatsuko growled.

Yamato made a dash for the door.

'Remember, I don't want her back – under any circumstances!' Hatsuko shouted. She paced to the other side of the room. 'Especially not now that my destiny is finally within reach,' she whispered under her breath.

★

Yamato cursed the traffic as he turned into the street opposite Harajuku railway station. He parked the car and fed the meter, then whispered harshly into the speaker on his wrist. 'Where is she now?'

Yuki stared at the screen. The blip was making its way along the street that Yamato said he was standing on. 'She should be close to you.'

Yamato looked around. All he could see were girls dressed in wacky costumes that would have looked more at home in Disneyland than on the streets of Tokyo. He scanned the other side of the street. 'I'm outside the crêperie. Which way?'

'She should be heading towards you from the direction of the station,' Yuki replied.

'She's not here. Unless she's taken to dressing as one of the Harajuku girls – and where would she have got the money for that?'

He turned around slowly. Among the throng was a group of Western tourists. Three were young girls, who were talking loudly. As they passed by, there was a loud crackle of static and Yamato's eardrum almost exploded. He leapt into the air and the tallest of the children, a blonde girl, laughed out loud.

A smaller child with long chocolate curls smiled at Yamato and darted around him.

'*Sumimasen,*' she said with a smile.

Yamato stared at her and Yuki's voice buzzed in his ear. 'Are you still outside the crêperie?'

Yamato rubbed his ear and shouted 'Yes' into his sleeve.

'Then she should be right next to you,' said Yuki. He wished he'd gone instead. Sometimes he wondered how his partner had acquired his position.

Yamato looked up and down the street. He peered through the shop window at the diners. There was no sign of her. The tracking device must be faulty – perhaps it was giving signals in the wrong locations now too, as well as switching off intermittently.

'She is *not* here,' he whispered savagely.

Chapter 17

The girls were delighted by their afternoon tea, with Millie declaring that Japanese crepes were definitely on par with the French. Michiko explained that the next stop on their tour was one of the local shops, where Alice-Miranda and her friends would be given a complete Harajuku makeover.

Inside the shop, five staff members swooped on the three girls and presented them with various outfits to try.

'While the children are playing dress-ups, I've

arranged some tea for the adults – through here.' Michiko pulled aside a green velvet curtain and revealed a perfect little room with a *tatami* floor.

'How lovely,' Cecelia said as she, Hugh and Ambrosia removed their shoes and followed the woman inside.

Michiko indicated that they should all sit down around a shiny black lacquered table. 'I will tell you about the tea ceremony,' she began.

Meanwhile, on the other side of the wall, Alice-Miranda, Millie and Jacinta were having a wonderful time choosing their outfits.

Alice-Miranda held up a blue dress with a sailor-style collar. 'What do you think of this one?'

'I like it,' Millie nodded. 'Isn't it like Sailor Moon's?'

'It will look much better when we accessorise,' one of the staff said. 'That is the key to Harajuku dressing.'

'What about this one?' Jacinta pulled out a pink confection that would have looked right at home on the miniature bride on top of a wedding cake.

'Pretty,' said Alice-Miranda.

'Hey, look what I found,' Millie called from the racks on the other side of the shop.

Alice-Miranda and Jacinta raced over to see.

'It's Itoshii Squirrel!' said Alice-Miranda, grinning.

'Ick, that awful creature.' Jacinta wrinkled her nose in disgust.

'It wasn't the squirrel's fault that the boy in the shop was horrible,' Alice-Miranda said. 'Come on, Jacinta, you have to admit he is adorable. Those eyes are huge.'

'Like yours,' Jacinta said.

'*Hai,*' said the girl who'd been helping Millie. 'Do you want to try it?'

Millie frowned. 'I think I'd feel a bit silly.'

As she spoke, a trio of Hello Kitties and a young man dressed as Astro Boy walked past the front window of the shop.

'No sillier than them.' Jacinta smiled and raised her eyebrows. 'I think anything goes in Harajuku.'

After lots of fussing and giggling the children were finally ready. Their own clothes had been wrapped and bagged as beautifully as if they'd just been bought and now the girls were waiting for the adults to return.

'How long does it take to drink a cup of tea?' Jacinta asked.

One of the women shook her head. 'It is not just drinking the tea. Tea ceremony is about preparing the tea, serving and then drinking it. It is very special green tea. I hope you get to go to tea ceremony too.'

Millie pulled a face. 'Oh, green tea is not my favourite.'

'Maybe we should practise walking in our outfits, like in a fashion show,' Jacinta suggested. 'So we can show off for the grown-ups.'

The staff nodded enthusiastically. One of them ran to another room and came back carrying a roll of carpet. She put it on the floor and unfurled a long red path for the children to use as their runway.

Just as Jacinta was about to lead off the rehearsal, the green curtain was pulled aside and her mother stepped out.

'Oh my goodness, look at you,' Ambrosia exclaimed.

Hugh and Cecelia followed her out.

'Where are the girls?' Hugh joked as he cast his eye over the children. 'Excuse me,' he said, turning to one of the shop assistants. 'Have you seen three children? A blonde, a redhead and a brunette.'

The girl bowed and smiled. 'I think you are very cheeky, Mr Hugh.'

'Yes, you're right about that,' said Cecelia.

Michiko turned to the children and smiled. 'Please show us your outfits.'

One of the shop assistants turned up the music and Jacinta strutted towards the adults.

She was wearing the pink lace dress with long pink boots and an enormous bow covering a curly pink wig. Heart-shaped sunglasses were perched on the tip of her nose and she had an armful of bracelets.

Ambrosia clapped wildly. 'You look amazing, darling.'

Jacinta grinned widely. *'Arigatou gozaimasu!'*

Alice-Miranda walked down the carpet next in her blue Sailor Moon costume, complete with little blue Mary-Jane shoes and frilly socks. She had a matching blue headband and pretty purse. At the end of their makeshift runway she stopped and pressed her left forefinger against her cheek.

Last of all Millie sprinted through the middle of the shop, her red cape flying out behind her. She was covered in fur and wore goggles painted with giant brown eyes.

'Oh my goodness, Millie, is that you under there?' Cecelia laughed.

'*Hai! Watashi wa* Itoshii Squirrel,' came Millie's muffled voice. She was beaming, although no one could see it beneath the costume.

The staff and parents clapped enthusiastically as the children took a bow.

Hugh Kennington-Jones glanced at his watch. 'It's getting late, I'm afraid. I think we should head back.'

Michiko nodded. '*Hai.* It has been a pleasure to meet you all.'

'Can we have some photographs first?' Millie asked. She ran to retrieve her camera from her backpack.

The children gathered together with the staff and Michiko and Hugh snapped away.

'*Arigatou,*' said Alice-Miranda as she shook hands with each of the shop assistants and Michiko. 'This afternoon has been so much fun. Thank you.'

'It was my pleasure,' Michiko said.

'Can we really keep the costumes?' Millie asked as the group headed for the door.

'*Hai,*' Michiko said. 'It is my shop and it is my pleasure.'

'So you're all staying like that for the trip home?' Hugh asked, shaking his head.

'Of course!' the girls chorused.

'Okay, I guess you'll blend in,' Hugh said.

'Until we get to the subway,' Alice-Miranda grinned. 'I haven't seen too many people outside of Harajuku dressed like us.'

'Mmm, you're right about that,' Hugh said. 'We could take taxis.'

'That would spoil our fun, Daddy. And look at how much trouble Michiko and the other ladies went to,' Alice-Miranda replied.

'Yeah,' Jacinta said. 'I think we should go out for dinner like this too.'

'Okay, if that's what you want,' Hugh nodded and grinned. The group thanked Michiko and her team for their generosity and bade them farewell, then gathered their parcels.

Hugh led the way out of the shop and onto the street. Within a couple of minutes, the children were attracting plenty of attention.

They heard *'kawaii'* over and over as people passed by.

'What does that mean?' Jacinta asked.

'Cute,' Alice-Miranda replied. It seemed that Millie was getting more *kawaii*s than anyone else. She was stopped several times to pose for photographs.

'So, do you see her?' Yuki hissed into the microphone.

Yamato shook his head. According to his partner, Kiko should have been inside the Harajuku store for the past hour or so, but he'd pressed his face against the window and seen only a group of foreigners being made up to look like characters.

'No, she is nowhere. That tracking device *must* be faulty.' Yamato watched as the group of westerners left the store.

He didn't see Alice-Miranda reach inside her dress and pull out her beautiful new necklace. 'Look Mummy, Daddy bought Millie and Jacinta and me presents this afternoon.' She held out her pendant for her mother to admire.

'Oh, darling, that's lovely. Millie, is yours the same?' she asked.

'No, mine's a cherry blossom branch,' the girl explained. Her necklace was hidden under her squirrel costume.

'Do you like mine?' Jacinta showed Cecelia her paper crane.

'That's gorgeous,' Cecelia grinned.

'I bought them from an antique dealer in the market near the inn,' said Hugh.

The children and adults reached the subway and disappeared onto the crowded train.

Back at the palace, Yuki stared at the screen. 'She's gone,' he said into the microphone.

Yamato exhaled. 'Well, you'd better hope that she reappears before Hatsuko does.'

Chapter 18

'Where are you, boy?' Obaasan called.

Kiko poked her head out of the bathhouse she'd been taken to clean an hour earlier, and peered into the hallway. There were two bathhouses at the rear of the building's ground floor – one for the men and the other for the women. Obaasan had handed her a mop, bucket and some spray, which Kiko worked out must be for the tiled walls. The liquid smelt sharp and made her head ache. After an hour immersed in the pungent odour, she was glad to hear the old woman's voice.

'Come, I need you to take tea to Ojiisan upstairs.'

Kiko wondered which Ojiisan the woman meant. There were many grandfathers in the house and she hoped it wasn't the one with the cane. She gathered her cleaning equipment and rushed to the kitchen. All the while, Kiko's eyes scanned every surface and crevice looking for her locket. She wondered if Obaasan had hidden it in her bedroom. There was another room at the front of the house, off the kitchen, which she hadn't been in either. It was on the corner near the alley and Tatsu was the only one she'd seen going in and out, but he always locked the door behind him.

Obaasan passed her a tray.

'Which room?' Kiko whispered.

'Upstairs, at the far end of the hall,' Obaasan replied. 'You look after him. He is special.'

It was the man Kiko had met earlier. At least he was friendly enough.

Kiko balanced the teapot and cup and walked up the timber staircase. She stepped carefully along the hall; the pot was so heavy her hands trembled. At the end of the passage, she placed the tray down and knocked on the door.

'Hello?' she called, hoping to hear his voice on the other side.

Kiko didn't want to barge in but she didn't want the tea to go cold either. There was a perfect temperature for serving and if she waited much longer it would be less than ideal.

'*Sumimasen*, I have your tea,' she said, pushing the door open.

The man was still sitting in his chair facing towards the window, exactly where he had been earlier.

Kiko picked up the tray, walked inside and set it down on a low table beside him.

'Would you like me to pour it?' she asked quietly, keeping her head low.

The man nodded. '*Hai.*'

Kiko bowed. She held the teapot and rotated it three times. Then she poured the tea, filling the cup a third of the way, then two-thirds and then an inch below the top. She passed it to the man and bowed.

'What is your name?' he asked.

Kiko gulped. 'Yoshi,' she whispered.

'How old are you?' the man asked. His hands trembled as he gripped the cup and liquid spilled over the sides and onto the small leather-bound book that was resting on his lap.

'Eleven,' Kiko replied. 'Would you like me to take that for you?' She pointed at the book.

He shook his head. 'No. Leave it.'

Kiko wondered what it was.

'You must not stay here,' he said, 'or you will die like everyone else.'

Kiko shifted uncomfortably. 'What do you mean, Ojiisan?'

The old man slurped his tea and set the cup back down.

'Would you like some more?' Kiko asked.

'No.'

Kiko noticed that every now and then his whole body trembled. She wondered what was wrong with him.

'You must leave this place,' the man said.

'But why do you stay?' Kiko asked.

'I have no choice. Perhaps you do not have a choice either.' He gripped the side of his chair and held tightly, as if trying to make the tremors stop.

'Boy, are you still up there?' Obaasan screeched from the bottom of the stairs. 'You get down here now.'

Kiko gathered up the tray and walked to the door.

The old man stared out the window. 'Go!' he said. 'Or you will be in trouble with the boss lady.'

He opened the leather-bound book on his lap. It was a photograph album. An exquisite young bride stared up at him.

Kiko glanced at it but he clutched the album to his chest. '*Arigatou*, Ojiisan,' she whispered, then walked as quickly as she could from the room and down the hall. Obaasan was waiting for her at the bottom of the stairs.

'What were you doing up there, boy? Making sushi? I have more jobs and you are lazy. Lazy!'

Kiko followed Obaasan back to the kitchen. She was good at blocking out the noise. Obaasan was no match for her Aunt Hatsuko. Besides, Obaasan at least praised her occasionally, which was more than could be said for her aunt.

Kiko was directed to stir a large pot of noodles on the stove. After a few minutes her arms felt like lead and she wondered how long she could keep it up.

'You tired, boy?' Obaasan said. She may not have been able to see too much but she was perceptive nonetheless.

Kiko nodded. '*Hai,*' she said softly.

'You're a good worker for a beginner. When you've had more practice you will be even better. I'm glad you sleep on my doorstep.'

'What is the matter with Ojiisan?' Kiko asked.

The old woman stood up on another small stool next to Kiko and scraped some meat into a sizzling pan. 'Ojiisan is just old,' she said.

'But he shakes,' Kiko said.

'His heart is broken,' Obaasan said. 'But I look after him and he has a good life. Better than if he had stayed out there.'

Out there. The words turned over in Kiko's mind. 'Out there' was where she needed to go. But first she had to find her necklace and get her mother's diary back.

Chapter 19

On their return journey to the inn, the children attracted a lot of attention. Hugh wondered if they'd ever get back, as people constantly stopped them for photographs. Finally they emerged from the station in Asakusa.

Alice-Miranda, Millie and Jacinta decided that they would change before dinner. Although being Itoshii Squirrel had been fun to start with, Millie was finding it difficult to breathe inside all that fur.

'Can you imagine how tired Uncle Lawrence

must get of being asked for photographs?' Alice-Miranda said as the children walked towards the inn.

'Yes, but he's a movie star,' Millie replied. 'He sort of brought it on himself, really.'

'And he's so handsome,' said Jacinta with a sigh. 'Who wouldn't want to have their photograph taken with Lawrence Ridley?'

Millie and Alice-Miranda giggled.

The adults were lagging behind when Alice-Miranda, Millie and Jacinta turned the corner into their street. The children walked past a large house, which Alice-Miranda noticed was built in the same style as their inn. Between the house and the inn was an alley. Like the inn, the house sat right on the edge of the road. In the downstairs window closest to the alley, the curtains were open a fraction, revealing a desk with a large screen on top of it.

'I wonder what they're watching,' Millie said as she noticed something playing on the screen.

'I haven't even thought about television since we've been here,' Alice-Miranda said. The girls' room at the inn was completely devoid of technology, apart from the toilet. 'I don't think we'd be able to understand much of it anyway.'

She and Jacinta kept walking but Millie peered through the window at the monitor. Then she stepped back and glanced up under the building's eaves. A tiny video camera stared back at her.

'Hey, look at this!' Millie rushed forward, grabbed Alice-Miranda's arm and pulled her back to the window. 'Look, on the screen.' Millie pointed.

Jacinta hurried back to join them.

'That's us on there,' Millie said, waving at the camera to prove her point.

Jacinta cupped her hands and stared through the window.

'So it is.' She looked up and spotted the camera. 'I wonder why they need surveillance. I thought Japan was a really safe place.'

'It is,' Alice-Miranda said, 'and we probably shouldn't be looking into people's windows.'

Millie stepped away but Jacinta continued to look.

Jacinta's jaw dropped. 'Oh my goodness, it's him! The kid from the Itoshii Squirrel shop just walked into that room.'

The boy looked up and caught Jacinta's gaze. She turned her head and pretended that she hadn't been watching him. He came forward and tapped on the glass. Jacinta jumped into the air. Millie and Alice-Miranda watched as he pointed at Jacinta and then ran his finger across his throat.

Millie's heart thumped. 'You little brat!' she called and shook her fist back at him.

'What did he do?' Jacinta whispered, still not wanting to turn around.

Millie was about to tell her when she spotted Alice-Miranda shaking her head.

'Nothing. He's just horrible,' said Millie, still staring at the boy.

'Come on, let's go.' Alice-Miranda grabbed Jacinta's hand and pulled her away.

'He wouldn't have recognised me in this outfit anyway,' Jacinta said.

Alice-Miranda wondered about that too. He certainly wouldn't have known it was Millie. Perhaps he was rude to everyone.

The boy shut the curtains just as the adults caught up to them.

'What were you looking at, girls?' Hugh asked.

'It was the boy from the shop near the temple,' Alice-Miranda explained.

'The one who upset Jacinta?' her father quizzed.

She nodded.

'Well, I might pay him and his father a visit after all.'

'*Who* upset Jacinta?' Ambrosia asked. It was the first she'd heard about it.

'Perhaps we should talk about it later, Daddy,' Alice-Miranda said pointedly.

Hugh looked from his daughter to Ambrosia and back. 'Okay, darling.'

The group arrived at the inn. 'Oh my goodness, look at you,' Aki exclaimed as the children flooded into the foyer. '*Kawaii.*'

'I think we've heard that about five thousand times between Harajuku and here,' Millie said. 'Itoshii Squirrel really is popular.'

'That's because he is so cute,' Aki grinned.

'What are we doing for dinner, then?' Hugh looked at Cecelia.

'I think we should stay in tonight,' Cecelia said. 'The children are tired and I'm afraid Ambrosia and I have more meetings tomorrow.'

'Here it is, then,' said Hugh. He turned to the girls. 'In the meantime, what would you three like to do until dinner?'

'Can we play a game?' Alice-Miranda asked.

'I can explain how to play one of the Japanese

board games,' Aki suggested. 'You could take it up to your room.'

Alice-Miranda and Jacinta nodded.

'That would be great,' Millie said, 'except I'll have to get changed first. I don't think squirrel paws will be very helpful at moving board pieces.'

Cecelia nodded. 'That sounds absolutely perfect. I think your father and I might have a rest, Alice-Miranda – I'm afraid we oldies don't have as much energy as you girls.'

'And I'm going to get a start on today's article,' Ambrosia said. 'How about we meet here at six-thirty for dinner?'

It was agreed. The adults wandered off, and Millie and Jacinta set about choosing a board game with Aki's help. Alice-Miranda was happy to let them decide – she was too distracted thinking about the boy next door.

★

In the girls' room, Millie scratched at her fur, eager to get out of the squirrel costume. She pulled off the head and took a deep breath.

'Remind me that I never want to get a job as a character at Disneyland,' she sighed.

'What did that boy next door do when I looked away?' Jacinta asked as she unfurled her futon.

'Um, he shook his fist,' Millie lied. She glanced over at Alice-Miranda, who nodded.

'So why do you think they have a surveillance camera over there?' Jacinta plonked down on the floor and took the lid off the game box.

'Who knows?' Alice-Miranda replied. 'Maybe they have a lot of money from the Itoshii Squirrel shop.'

'Yes, that's probably it,' Jacinta agreed as she set up the board.

Alice-Miranda wondered too. She had a strange feeling about that boy and the house across the alleyway.

Chapter 20

The next morning, Kiko hovered in the kitchen, hoping that Obaasan would send her to the market. She had already served breakfast and finished the washing up. She'd decided she had to prove how reliable she was, so that the old woman would return her backpack and let her out to run errands. Then she would make her escape and find her grandparents' house.

Kiko noticed that the old woman's face was more contorted than usual and she was muttering something under her breath. 'Are, are you all right, Obaasan?'

'Does it look like I am all right?' the woman snapped.

'Is there something I can do?' Kiko asked. 'The shopping, perhaps?'

'No!' Obaasan growled. 'You can do your work and leave me alone.'

Kiko drew in a deep breath. 'But you are upset and I am only trying to help.'

'Okay, boy. If you are so happy to help, you can clean the room upstairs.'

That wasn't what Kiko was hoping for.

'Which one?'

'First on the left. Where Tanaka-san used to be.'

Kiko was silent, wondering what the old woman meant.

Obaasan turned and walked closer. 'Don't be surprised. Old people die all the time.'

Kiko wanted to retract her offer and stay in the kitchen or, better still, go to the laundry.

As she was thinking, the kitchen door flew open and Obaasan's son, Tatsu, entered.

'I need to open the shop,' he grumbled.

'You need to make some arrangements first,'

Obaasan tsked. 'Sit down and I will get you some tea, then you can make the call.'

The man looked at Kiko and sneered. 'What's your name, boy?'

Kiko kept her eyes low. 'Yoshi.'

'Where did you come from?' he asked, walking closer.

'The alley,' Kiko said quietly.

'Don't get smart with me!' The man grabbed her chin and held her face high. 'You don't look like a street child.'

His breath stank like rancid fish and Kiko had to stop herself from gagging.

'Show me your hands.' He pulled Kiko's arms forward. 'So soft and smooth. You're a runaway. Where are you from?'

Kiko pulled her arms back and clenched her fists beside her. 'Nowhere.'

'Well, Yoshi from nowhere, just remember: you see nothing and you hear nothing in this house.'

Kiko fixed her gaze on his pockmarked face. '*Hai,*' she whispered.

The man turned and walked back to the table where Obaasan set a teacup in front of him.

'What are you waiting for, boy? Take this.'

Obaasan handed her a small bucket with cleaning cloths and a broom.

Kiko walked out of the kitchen towards the stairs. She would do as she was told, for now.

✳

Charlotte, Lawrence and Lucas arrived at the *ryokan* just after breakfast. As always, Alice-Miranda greeted her aunt with a peppering of kisses, although she insisted that Charlotte not pick her up this time, because the woman was six months pregnant with twins.

Cecelia had been concerned that her sister might not want to fly but Charlotte had declared she was feeling better than ever, apart from being tired, and her doctor had given his permission.

The adults had some tea and the girls showed Lucas upstairs to his room. He was next door to them and his father and stepmother were on the other side.

'This place is mad,' Lucas said.

Millie winked. 'Wait until you use the toilet.'

The girls made a great show of explaining their new-found knowledge of Japanese customs.

'There's a communal bathhouse downstairs at the end of the corridor,' Jacinta said.

'Communal?' Lucas asked. 'Doesn't that mean all in together?'

Jacinta grinned and raised her eyebrows. 'Yes.'

Lucas gulped. 'Can you wear your swimmers?'

'Na-ah.' Jacinta shook her head. 'Birthday suits only.'

'Yeah, we're going later on,' Millie teased. 'If you stay in the inn, you have to go. It's one of the rules.'

Lucas blushed. The three girls exchanged glances – they were enjoying watching Lucas squirm.

Hugh Kennington-Jones walked towards them. 'Were the girls telling you about the bathhouse? What do you think, Lucas – are you up for it?'

The boy shook his head. 'I . . . I don't think so.'

'It's all right, mate, it's just us men.' Hugh slapped him on the back.

'Oh, really?' Lucas said. 'That's not what I heard.'

Hugh looked around at the trio of giggling girls behind them. 'You cheeky things. You know, I did see a public bathhouse down the road – with mixed baths. Perhaps you'd like to go there instead? I could give that a try.'

'No way!' Millie flinched and pulled a face.

'So, you're not keen after all, Millie. It's all right, Lucas. We blokes will stick together.'

'Are we going out with Ambrosia today?' Alice-Miranda asked her father as they walked back along the hallway. The previous evening there had been talk of the girls visiting a kimono maker with her while Cecelia and Charlotte met with some suppliers.

'Yes, if you'd like to.'

Alice-Miranda nodded. 'What are you going to do, Daddy?'

'I'm going to take Lucas and Lawrence for a walk around here and then we're going to meet you and Ambrosia at the hotel where Dolly's giving her speech. I've checked with the organisers and we're welcome to sit up the back. I thought the old girl might like some moral support. It's only for an hour or so and then we can go and see the Meiji Shrine that we missed yesterday afternoon, and maybe the Tokyo Tower too.'

The children agreed that it sounded like a great plan.

Ambrosia arrived in reception. 'Okay, girls, we'd better get going.'

'See you at the hotel at two,' Hugh said.

The girls followed Jacinta's mother outside.

'How are we getting there?' Millie asked.

'We'll walk. According to the map Aki drew for me it's just a couple of blocks away, towards the temple.'

Jacinta glanced at the house where they'd spotted the boy the previous evening. 'Look at that,' she said.

A black van was parked out the front and a gurney was being wheeled into the street. A pair of slippered feet was poking out from beneath a white sheet.

'Is that . . . is that a body?' Millie whispered, her eyes wide.

'Oh, how sad.' Alice-Miranda was looking at the two attendants. A reed-thin man followed them out the front door.

'That's him,' Jacinta said. 'The man from the squirrel shop.'

'Yes, that's him all right,' Millie agreed. 'I'll never forget that face.'

'So he's the man who accused you of stealing?' Ambrosia asked, adjusting her sunglasses. Millie and Jacinta had taken great delight in explaining everything during dinner the previous evening.

Jacinta nodded.

The woman drew herself up and flicked her silken brunette tresses over her shoulders. Before the children knew what was happening, Ambrosia Headlington-Bear marched down the road on her towering heels.

The attendants closed the door of the van and hopped in. The engine started and the vehicle pulled away from the kerb.

'What's your mother doing?' Millie asked.

'I think she's going to speak to him.'

'But they've just had a death in the family,' Alice-Miranda said. 'It might not be the best time.'

'Mummy!' Jacinta called, but Ambrosia had already reached her target.

'Excuse me.' Ambrosia tapped the remaining man on his shoulder.

He spun around and stared at her.

'I believe that you wrongly accused my daughter of stealing in your shop yesterday,' Ambrosia said.

The man caught sight of the girls racing up behind the woman.

'Ambrosia,' Alice-Miranda interrupted. 'I think he might have other things on his mind.'

Ambrosia turned to face the child. 'Yes, I'm aware of that, but I just want to let him know that

I don't appreciate him accusing Jacinta of stealing.'
She turned back to face him. 'My daughter is not
a thief and I think your son, who quite obviously
set her up, owes her an apology. And you too, for
that matter.'

A sneer crept onto his face.

'What's that look for?' Ambrosia demanded.

The curtains moved in the window behind him
and Jacinta spotted the young boy's face peering out.

'There he is!' Jacinta shouted.

'Right, I'm going to have a word with that child.'
Ambrosia stepped past the man and walked to the
front door.

'Hey! Where are you going?' he snarled in
English.

'Oh no, Mummy, please come back.' Jacinta
had been horrified at being wrongly accused, but
she was even more upset at the thought of her
mother barging into someone's home and telling off
their son – especially if there'd just been a tragedy
in the family.

Ambrosia pushed the door and it swung open.
She marched into the foyer, her shoes clip-clopping
on the timber floor.

'Where are you, you horrid little monster?'

Ambrosia bellowed. She turned right and pushed through another door into the kitchen.

A voice screeched from the hallway and then a tiny woman shuffled through the kitchen door and stood in front of Ambrosia.

'What are you doing in my house?' she demanded. Then she looked down at Ambrosia's feet. 'You wear shoes in my house! Who are you?'

Ambrosia Headlington-Bear looked at the tiny woman with the wild eyes and began to rethink her actions.

Alice-Miranda, Millie and Jacinta had chased Ambrosia inside – but fortunately they'd all remembered to remove their shoes first. The man who'd been out the front was now at the old lady's side.

'Wow!' Millie's eyes were on stalks. 'Look at all those squirrels,' she gasped as she glanced around the kitchen. 'This place is insane.'

'No, my mother is insane,' Jacinta whispered and shook her head.

'I'm sorry, madam, but I want to speak to the boy in the window of that room through there.' Ambrosia tried to retain her fury, but all the while her cheeks were alight with shame.

'What boy?' the old woman asked.

'That boy.' Jacinta pointed at the chubby lad, who was peering out from around the door.

'Taro!' the old woman shouted. 'What are you doing in there?'

The boy scurried out and stopped in front of his grandmother. The old woman spoke quickly in Japanese. He shouted back at her and fled from the kitchen.

'What are you doing in my house? He is gone. You need to go too!' The old woman shuffled forward and waved her hands at Ambrosia.

The man with the pockmarked face narrowed his eyes. 'You must leave now.' He strode over to the door that Taro had come from, pulled it shut and locked it with a key.

Alice-Miranda and Millie exchanged curious looks. 'I wonder what's so valuable in there,' Millie whispered.

Alice-Miranda had been thinking the same thing.

'I . . . I'm sorry, I don't know what came over me,' Ambrosia stuttered. 'It's just that your grandson did something yesterday that upset my daughter.'

'What did fat boy do?'

'He put something into Jacinta's pocket at the

shop, and then I believe it was you –' Ambrosia looked at the man beside her – 'who accused her of stealing.'

Obaasan glanced up at the man. She started speaking furiously in Japanese. His shoulders slumped and he skulked from the room. She turned to Ambrosia. 'You need to leave. I have things to do and you are wearing shoes in my house.'

It was clear that Ambrosia wasn't going to get anywhere with the woman.

'Come on girls, let's go.' She bowed several times and turned to leave.

Millie and Jacinta followed Ambrosia. But Alice-Miranda stayed behind.

'*Sumimasen,*' the child said.

The old woman squinted and a thousand more wrinkles appeared.

'I'm so sorry that we barged into your house and I'm very sorry for your loss.'

'She is a crazy person,' the old woman said, pointing towards the door. Then a puzzled look settled on her face. 'What loss?'

'We just saw someone being taken away in a van under a sheet.'

'Oh, you mean the dead old man,' the woman said, flicking her hand in the air.

'I'm sure you must be upset,' Alice-Miranda said.

'*Hai*, of course I am upset. Now I need to find someone to sleep in his room.'

Alice-Miranda took the curious statement in. She looked around, trying to work out what this place was.

'I'm sorry, I haven't even introduced myself properly. My name is Alice-Miranda Highton-Smith-Kennington-Jones.'

The old woman wrinkled her nose. 'That is nice for you. But I don't care. You need to leave my house.'

'What may I call you?'

'Obaasan,' the woman replied. 'Hurry up. Get out. I have work to do and you talk too much.'

The old woman shuffled forward. She was only a bit taller than the child herself. Obaasan pushed open the kitchen door and Alice-Miranda walked through. She was about to leave when she noticed a stream of elderly people shuffling down the end of the hall, like a geriatric caterpillar.

'Alice-Miranda!' Millie called from the front porch. 'Hurry up, we need to get going.'

Alice-Miranda bowed. 'It was a pleasure to meet you, Obaasan.'

'Well, of course it was. But I can't say the same about you.' The old woman ushered Alice-Miranda out. The child barely had time to collect her shoes before the door slammed in her face.

Obaasan turned and shuffled back towards the kitchen.

'Yoshi!' she called. Kiko scurried from the sitting room off the back hall, where she had been tidying up. 'I need you to go to the market.'

Kiko tried to suppress her smile. *'Hai, hai.'*

'Come with me and I'll get the list.' Obaasan walked across the hallway to the front room. She took a key from her apron and unlocked the door that her son had pulled shut. Kiko stood in the doorway and observed the row of filing cabinets lining the walls and the desk with its large screen.

'My son is addicted to games. He spends way too much time in here,' the old woman said, shaking her head.

Kiko stared at the screen. She flinched when she realised it was showing Taro walking down the street. It wasn't a video game at all.

Obaasan sat down and began to scribble on a piece of paper. 'Turn around and face the other way, boy,' she said.

Kiko obeyed, wondering what the old woman was doing and why she wasn't allowed to look. She heard several clicks.

Kiko couldn't help herself. She turned quickly to snatch a peek. Obaasan was bent over with her head inside a cupboard. The old woman was pulling on something heavy – a door. Kiko realised that the clicking was the same noise she'd heard once at home, when she had been taken to see her mother's jewels. Obaasan had her head inside a safe.

Obaasan pulled out a wad of money. She peeled off a couple of notes, returned the bundle and closed the door. Kiko turned around and pretended not to have seen a thing.

'Take this. Go to the shop opposite Itoshii Squirrel and tell that man I want the freshest vegetables he has or I will be taking my business elsewhere. His cabbage was rotten last week.'

Kiko reached for the money. She rubbed her fingers over its surface and looked closely at the notes.

'What are you doing now?' Obaasan squinted through her glasses and gave Kiko a shove. 'Haven't you ever seen a thousand yen note before?'

Kiko smiled to herself. No, she hadn't.

Chapter 21

'Well, that was awkward,' Millie mumbled. 'And what is that place? Squirrels, security cameras, locked rooms, dead bodies? Do you think they could be Yakuza?'

Alice-Miranda frowned. 'Gangsters? With squirrels? I don't think so. What do you know about the Yakuza, anyway?'

'There was a little bit about them in my guidebook,' Millie said. 'Apparently they run lots of respectable businesses that cover up their criminal activities. Maybe Itoshii Squirrel is a front for a gang.'

'You really are becoming a fount of international wisdom,' Alice-Miranda grinned. 'With a very good imagination.'

The three girls ran to catch up to Ambrosia, who was stalking away at top speed.

'Mummy, what were you thinking?' Jacinta rebuked.

'I don't know. When you told me what happened at the shops and then he was right there, I . . . I just wanted to make him understand that he couldn't go around doing that sort of thing to people, especially not children,' Ambrosia replied.

'Thank you for sticking up for me, but next time, please don't do it when someone has just *died*,' Jacinta said.

Ambrosia smoothed the front of her trousers and pulled her handbag over her shoulder. 'Sorry, girls. I don't know what came over me. Let's just get to our appointment.'

Alice-Miranda smiled at her. 'Maybe your timing was a little off, but you were thinking about Jacinta, and that's a good thing.'

Ambrosia looked at the tiny girl. 'Yes, I suppose

you're right about that, on all counts. I'm sure we're going to have a lovely day,' she said with a decisive nod. 'But I could do with a coffee.'

As luck would have it, there was a vending machine on the next corner. The girls had been surprised to see them all around the city: on street corners, in alleyways, at railway stations. They contained everything from chocolate bars and chips to beer and cigarettes. Millie had decided that Japanese children must be a lot more responsible than children in most other countries. It seemed that anyone could put money in and get the goods out, but apparently it was unheard of for youngsters to raid the machines for anything they weren't allowed to have.

As the girls walked past, Millie peered inside the glass case. 'Ambrosia, I can get you a coffee,' she announced.

The woman looked around the street. There were no cafes anywhere.

Millie pointed. 'In there.'

The others looked into the machine and were surprised to see cans of hot coffee next to the usual varieties of soft drink.

'Oh, I don't think so,' said Ambrosia with a grimace. 'I've never had coffee from a can and I don't fancy starting now.'

Millie was disappointed.

Ambrosia pulled the map out of her handbag. She looked at the page and then at the street around them. 'Oh dear.'

'What's the matter?' Alice-Miranda asked.

'I think we've come too far.' The woman smacked her lips together and looked around for someone they could ask for directions.

Alice-Miranda noticed a boy in a baseball cap walking towards them. *'Sumimasen,'* Alice-Miranda called out as he drew closer.

The boy had his head down and seemed to ignore her. Jacinta strode over to block his path.

'Excuse me,' she said.

The boy had no option but to stop.

'Do you think you might be able to help us, just quickly?' She pointed at the map, which her mother passed to her. 'You see, we're supposed to be here and we really can't work out where we are.'

The boy gulped and looked at the girl's map.

Kiko's mind was racing. She was almost lost herself, and relying on a simple map Obaasan had scrawled for her. She pulled it out of her pocket and studied it, then looked back at the map the blonde girl was holding.

She pointed to where she thought they were at

that moment. Alice-Miranda stepped forward to take a look.

'*Arigatou gozaimasu*,' said the girl with the chocolate curls. '*Watashi wa* Alice-Miranda *desu*. What's your name? I'm sorry I don't know how to ask that in Japanese.'

Kiko glanced up. 'Yoshi.'

'That's a lovely name,' Alice-Miranda said. She noticed that the boy had a deep scar just under his left eye. Then she realised that he was staring at her neck. 'Oh, it's lovely, isn't it?' She held the pendant out for him to see. 'My father bought it for me yesterday from an antique shop in the market.' Alice-Miranda wondered if any of what she'd just said made sense to the boy.

But Kiko understood perfectly. Her English was almost as good as her Japanese. Her aunt had insisted that she learn and had spent many days speaking nothing else to her.

'It's lovely,' Kiko whispered.

'Oh, you can speak English,' Alice-Miranda said gratefully. 'That's wonderful. I'm afraid that we're all pretty hopeless with our Japanese.'

'Which market?' the child asked.

'Sorry?' Alice-Miranda frowned.

'Where did your father buy it?'

'Just near the temple. Daddy thought it would be a lovely memento of our holiday. Millie and Jacinta have different ones.'

Millie held hers forward and so did Jacinta, but Kiko's eyes did not stray from Alice-Miranda.

Kiko's mind was racing. Someone had taken her necklace and sold it at the market. It was probably that revolting fat boy, Taro, or his horrible father. She didn't think Obaasan would have done it – goodness knows she didn't need the money. But she couldn't just ask for it back from the girl. That would be risking too much.

'Are you staying close by?' Kiko asked.

'*Hai*, we're at the Sadachiyo Ryokan,' Alice-Miranda replied.

Kiko remembered that was the name of the place next door to Obaasan's. She had no idea how she was going to get the necklace back but she had to try. 'Are you in Tokyo for long?' she asked.

'We're staying until the end of the week, then we're off to a place in the mountains called Tsumago.' Alice-Miranda gushed.

Kiko nodded. At least she had a few more days to work out what to do. The little girl seemed nice enough. Perhaps if she explained . . . Kiko shook the thought from her mind. If she explained, she would be found and sent home. And that wasn't going to happen, no matter what.

Ambrosia Headlington-Bear looked at her watch. She'd been studying the map and working out which way to go.

'Well, thank you. *Arigatou*,' Ambrosia told the lad. 'Come on, girls, we really must get going or we'll be late.'

'*Sayonara*,' the three girls called and then turned to follow Ambrosia.

Kiko watched as the group disappeared around the corner. She had to have that necklace back. She'd never stolen anything in her life, but surely since it had been hers to begin with, taking it back wouldn't actually be stealing at all.

Chapter 22

Ambrosia and the girls were running late by the time they departed the kimono maker's studio. The designer had insisted that the girls try on some of the beautiful garments which, unbeknown to them, she was planning to send to the inn as gifts. Ambrosia thought it would be a wonderful surprise.

'Imagine how many silkworms it took to spin that delicate fabric,' Alice-Miranda said.

'Not to mention how long it takes to dye and then create the embroidery. I never realised it was such a complicated process,' Millie said. 'It's awful to think that kimono making is a dying art.'

'I loved them,' Jacinta said. 'But I suppose we wouldn't really get to wear kimonos at home, unless there was a fancy dress party.'

As they arrived at Dolly's hotel, Ambrosia paid the fare and Alice-Miranda dashed out of the taxi and into the marble and glass foyer with Millie and Jacinta hot on her heels.

Alice-Miranda scooted towards the concierge desk. '*Sumimasen.* Could you please tell us where the Invention and Innovation conference is taking place?'

The concierge, a young man with kind eyes, smiled and said, 'Of course. It is in the Chrysanthemum Auditorium on the level below.'

'*Arigatou,*' the three girls called as Ambrosia caught up to them.

The woman glanced at her watch. It was a minute to two and they were meant to be there at least ten minutes ago. 'Oh dear. I hope they let us in.'

The foursome raced towards the elevator. Alice-Miranda spotted a spiral staircase and decided that would be quicker. They ran down the stairs and across the foyer towards the double doors. Hugh was standing outside looking up and down and glancing at his watch. A security man was beside him.

'Hello Daddy,' Alice-Miranda called. 'Sorry we're late. We couldn't get away – and it was such fun.'

'Oh, thank goodness. They were about to close the doors.'

Hugh nodded at the fellow at the entrance, who ushered the group inside. Lawrence and Lucas were sitting in the back row with several empty seats beside them. The room was a large auditorium with tiered seating running down to the stage.

Ambrosia sat beside Lawrence with Jacinta and Millie next, then Alice-Miranda and her father at the end closest to the aisle. They'd just got settled when a tall man walked to the podium.

'*Konnichiwa*,' he said and bowed. '*Watashi wa* Nobu Taguchi *desu*.'

Jacinta leaned across Millie and whispered to Alice-Miranda, 'Is this whole thing going to be in Japanese?'

'I don't think so. Mrs Oliver's giving the speech,' said Alice-Miranda. 'As far as I know, she doesn't speak a word.'

'I would like to introduce our very special guest,' Mr Taguchi said in English.

'Oh, thank goodness,' Jacinta said.

He gave a short introduction about Dolly and her inventions. There was some talk about her lack of formal training and how that hadn't impeded her excellence and inventiveness, which was now world renowned. Then the man said the most peculiar thing.

'I have been most impressed by Mrs Oliver's grasp of the Japanese language. If I didn't know better I would say that she converses as though it were her mother tongue.'

Alice-Miranda glanced up at her father, who was looking puzzled. 'What's he talking about, Daddy? I've never heard Mrs Oliver speak Japanese.'

'No, me neither,' he replied, shaking his head. 'That's a mystery to me.'

'I welcome Mrs Dolly Oliver.' The man bowed and Mrs Oliver walked across the stage. Alice-Miranda noticed that her face was red and even her trademark curls weren't quite as helmet-like as usual.

'*Arigatou,*' Dolly mumbled and looked out at the audience. She placed a black folder onto the lectern and turned the first page. Dolly cleared her throat and began her speech. 'Your excellency, the Grand Chamberlain, honoured guests, ladies and gentlemen.' She glanced up and spotted Alice-Miranda in the back row. 'And boys and girls. It is an honour to be here today to speak to you about the development of JAW – which stands for Just Add Water.

'Before I tell you about the technical aspects of the work, I'd like to say that none of this would have been possible without the support of my employers, Mr Hugh Kennington-Jones and his wife Cecelia Highton-Smith, who not only encourage me to spend my spare time dabbling, but have also built me an extraordinary laboratory in which to do my work. I like to think that's because Mr Hugh recognised my potential, but perhaps it had more to do with the plumbing issues I was causing upstairs.'

There was a titter of laughter around the room. Hugh grinned and gave Dolly the thumbs up from the back row.

'Is that true, Daddy?' Alice-Miranda whispered.

'You'd better believe it, darling. I once came downstairs to find Dolly covered in some goopy substance that was bubbling out of the kitchen drains and all over the floor.'

The audience sat enthralled by Dolly's tales, although when she started to discuss the more technical elements, Jacinta began to yawn. Millie commenced a silent game of 'Who threw the devon?', in which she counted the number of men in the room sporting a large round bald spot on the back of their head.

'It has been a pleasure to be here and I thank the Ministry for their very kind invitation to speak,' Dolly finished. She stepped back from the podium and bowed.

There was an eruption of enthusiastic applause as Nobu took to the stage and asked the audience to once again thank Mrs Oliver for her incredible work. Dolly fiddled with the folder and began to walk towards the steps.

'Not so quickly, Mrs Oliver. Please do not run away. Would you mind if we took some questions from the floor?' Nobu asked.

Dolly's lips formed a thin line.

'Of course, if you would like to ask her in Japanese, I'm sure that will be fine too,' the man said.

Dolly gulped. Small beads of perspiration appeared on her temples and a red rash crept up her neck.

Alice-Miranda leaned over to her father. 'Daddy, is Mrs Oliver all right?'

'I'm not sure, darling,' Hugh replied.

A sea of hands shot up around the room.

'May I have a glass of water?' Dolly asked her host. She tugged at the collar on her blazer and wiped her brow.

'Mrs Oliver?' The man walked over and spoke quietly to her, then turned around and addressed the audience. 'I'm afraid that Mrs Oliver is not feeling well, so if you could save your questions, we will ask her to join our final panel for the day. Of course, she will be with us for the rest of the conference too, so there will be many opportunities to chat with her.'

'Thank you,' Dolly mouthed. She disappeared off the side of the stage.

'We will now break for afternoon tea. If I could ask you to stand while our official visitors leave first, then please join us in the upstairs foyer,' the man directed.

A tall, particularly handsome Japanese man led the way, followed by two men in black suits.

He smiled and nodded at the delegates as he walked up the stairs towards the back of the auditorium. As he neared the top, he stopped.

'Hugh?' The man looked at Hugh Kennington-Jones and smiled widely.

'Kenzo?' Hugh frowned.

'My goodness, I heard your name mentioned by Mrs Oliver but I had no idea that you would be here,' the man replied. 'Please, would you be my guest for afternoon tea?'

'Oh, I'm afraid it's not just me.' Hugh motioned towards Alice-Miranda and the girls, Ambrosia, Lucas and Lawrence. 'I brought along a cheer squad.'

Kenzo nodded at the group. 'There will be an abundance of food.'

'Well, as long we won't be stopping you from mingling with the delegates?' said Hugh.

Kenzo shook his head. 'No. I have a private room. It will be very dull on my own. Please, come with me.'

Hugh grinned. 'We'd be honoured.'

Chapter 23

Kiko couldn't stop thinking about the children she'd met on her way to the market. That pendant around the little girl's neck had to be hers. The girl couldn't know that it had been stolen and Kiko couldn't alert anyone to the fact either. But one way or another she had to get it back.

When she'd returned from the store, Obaasan had been busy on the telephone in the kitchen. A little while later the doorbell rang and Kiko was sent to let in an old woman who had arrived in a taxi.

She had grey hair and brown eyes, and carried only a small suitcase. Obaasan guided her away upstairs before Kiko could learn the woman's name or how long she was planning to stay.

Now Kiko was doing some more washing in the basement laundry. Obaasan's shrill voice screamed her name, so Kiko raced upstairs.

'What is it?' she panted.

Obaasan was standing in the kitchen leaning against the sink and clenching her fists. 'We have another one.'

'Another one?' Kiko asked cautiously.

'He told me he was planning to go soon, but I didn't think he meant today.'

Kiko gasped. She hoped Obaasan didn't mean the Ojiisan at the end of the hallway.

'Who is it?' Kiko asked.

'The grumpy old curmudgeon who sat at the end of the table. But you know, I liked him. He made me laugh and he didn't smell so bad either.' Obaasan sighed. 'He could have waited until tomorrow. One a month is enough for me and now we have two in a day.'

'Does his family know?' asked Kiko.

Obaasan shook her head. 'He has no family.

That's why he came here and I looked after him so well.'

'You are a good friend,' the child said quietly.

'Do you think so?'

Kiko wondered if she was going to have to pack away the man's things and clean the room, just as she had earlier.

Obaasan looked at the clock on the wall.

'Yoshi, go and make tea for Ojiisan in the room at the end of the hall,' Obaasan instructed. 'I will make some phone calls.'

The child did as she was told. She much preferred to make tea over cleaning another dead person's room.

A few minutes later she carried the tea tray carefully upstairs and knocked at the door. She called out but there was no answer. Kiko put the tray down and slid open the door, then took the tray to the table. As usual, he was in the chair facing the window, but now his eyes were closed. Kiko's heart thumped. She'd heard once that bad things happened in threes.

'Ojiisan,' she whispered. 'Would you like me to pour your tea?'

He didn't move. Kiko leaned in closer.

'Ojiisan,' she said a little louder.

He snorted and sat upright. Kiko leapt into the air.

'What? What is it?' he demanded.

'Sorry, Ojiisan. I just had to check.'

'Check what? That I was breathing?' He peered at the girl.

Kiko didn't reply.

'You can let that silly old woman know that there is life in me yet.'

Kiko nodded. She picked up the teapot and began to pour exactly the same way she had done the day before.

The old man studied her. 'Why does Obaasan think you are a boy?'

Kiko froze. 'I am a boy,' she whispered.

'Then I am a teenager,' the old man replied, raising his fuzzy eyebrows.

Kiko's head spun and she reached out to steady herself.

'Don't worry. I won't tell the old witch. You must have your reasons. We all have our reasons for being here and it is none of her worry as long as you do your work.'

Kiko exhaled. 'How did you know?' she asked.

'You have slender hands. They remind me of my

daughter,' he said. 'And you don't pour tea like any boy I have ever seen.'

Kiko inspected her fingers. It was true – they were long. She had taught herself to play the *koto* and had begged her aunt for lessons, but they were not forthcoming. Hatsuko did not like music.

'Is your daughter close by?' Kiko asked.

The man closed his eyes and brushed away a tear. His lip trembled. 'My daughter is gone.'

'I'm sorry. It is none of my business,' Kiko said, and quickly poured some more tea.

Sunlight streamed through the windows, bathing the man in light. He sipped his tea and sat in silence.

Kiko retreated and turned to walk back along the hall. For the second time that day, one of the old people was being carried downstairs, never to return.

Chapter 24

'Who is that man, Daddy?' Alice-Miranda asked, tugging at her father's sleeve as the group followed Kenzo and his minders.

'I'll introduce you in a minute, darling.'

They were directed across the giant foyer and into a smaller room, where a long table laden with colourful food took centre stage.

Once they were inside with the doors shut, Kenzo walked over and shook Hugh's hand. Then, to everyone's surprise, the two men embraced.

'How long has it been?' Kenzo stepped backwards and looked at Hugh with a huge grin.

'I can't recall. Probably the end of university, I should think. Excuse my ignorance, but can I assume that you're now the Grand Chamberlain?' Hugh asked.

'Yes, who would have thought it? I never imagined I'd be working with the Emperor, but here I am.'

'Well done, old chap. I can't believe I hadn't caught up on that news.' Hugh shook his head, then realised that the rest of the group was looking at them in puzzlement.

'I'd like you all to meet Kenzo Aoki. We spent years together at boarding school and then studied some of the same subjects at university. Kenzo is now the Grand Chamberlain of the Imperial family.'

Kenzo smiled and bowed.

'Allow me to introduce everyone. This is my daughter, Alice-Miranda, and her friends Millie and Jacinta and Jacinta's mother, Ambrosia Headlington-Bear,' said Hugh, gesturing to each in turn.

'It is a pleasure to meet you all,' Kenzo bowed again. He looked at the chrysanthemum hanging around Alice-Miranda's neck. 'What a pretty pendant. I think the young princess has one just like it.'

'*Arigatou*, Mr Kenzo,' said Alice-Miranda. 'Daddy bought it for me yesterday in the market.'

'And this is my brother-in-law, Lawrence Ridley, and his son, Lucas.'

'Did you say Lawrence Ridley?' Kenzo asked as he shook hands with the man.

'Yes, that's right,' Lawrence replied, smiling his dazzling smile.

'He's famous,' Jacinta piped up.

Kenzo grinned. 'You are the movie star?'

'Absolutely,' Jacinta replied, her eyes dreamy.

'Darling, I do think Lawrence can speak for himself,' Ambrosia chided.

Jacinta wrinkled her nose at her mother.

'I don't know about the star bit but I do get to spend my days pretending to be someone else, and having way too much fun in the process,' Lawrence explained.

'I know someone who would be thrilled to meet you,' Kenzo said.

'Everyone's thrilled to meet him. I was so excited I thought I was going to faint the first time and then I kept saying lots of silly things because, well, look at him,' Jacinta babbled.

The rest of the group stared at her.

'Seriously, do you know what a stalker you sound like right now?' Millie asked, grinning.

Jacinta blushed. 'Sorry, I didn't mean to sound weird.'

Lucas rolled his eyes. 'You're crazy,' he grinned.

'Girls, why don't we get something to eat?' Ambrosia suggested. She was worried about what her daughter might come out with next.

'Yes, please go ahead,' said Kenzo. 'There is much to try.'

'I'm starving,' Millie groaned.

'I hope it's normal food,' Jacinta whispered.

'Of course it will be normal,' Alice-Miranda said. 'For Japan, that is.'

Jacinta shuddered. 'That's exactly what I'm afraid of.'

Millie took Alice-Miranda's hand and the girls walked towards the buffet table.

'Are you in Tokyo for long?' Kenzo asked Hugh.

'We arrived on Sunday evening and we're staying in the city for the week, and then planning a bit of mountain sightseeing after that. Cecelia and her sister are working, and Ambrosia is too for most of the time, so Lawrie and I get to play with the kids.'

Kenzo tapped his forefinger to his lip. 'Very interesting.'

'What are you thinking, old chap?'

Kenzo lowered his voice. 'I don't know if you're aware that the Emperor has not been at all well in recent years. But one of the things that gives him great joy is watching films. He has especially enjoyed movies starring Mr Ridley.'

'I'm sure Lawrence would be happy to write him a note or sign something and have it sent over,' Hugh replied.

'I was thinking more than that. Perhaps you would like to bring the family for a meal at the Imperial Palace?' Kenzo suggested. 'I'm afraid at such short notice it would be very informal.'

'Oh, Kenzo, that sounds fabulous but I wouldn't want you to go to any trouble,' Hugh replied. 'I was reading something recently about the extraordinary bureaucracy one has to negotiate to arrange anything for the royal family, so please don't fuss on our account.'

'It will be no bother. This could be just the thing we need. And besides, the Emperor's sister is quite besotted with Mr Ridley so it would elevate me in her eyes too.' Kenzo raised his eyebrows.

'Oh, I see, you old charmer.' Hugh smiled. 'So, you and the princess?'

'That torch has been alight for many years now but my hopes fade with each passing year,' Kenzo replied. 'Your visit might even bring the young princess out too.'

'It sounds like you've got some battles over there,' Hugh said.

His friend nodded. 'Some days I think my life would be a lot less complicated if I had taken a job in a bank.'

'I'm sure it's not as bad as all that,' said Hugh. 'Besides, you live in a palace, and how many staff do you have?'

'At last count I believe it was . . . twelve hundred.' Kenzo shook his head, as if shocked by the number himself.

'Twelve hundred!' Hugh exclaimed. 'And how many members of the family live in the palace these days?'

'Now I will be truly embarrassed.' Kenzo cast his eyes downwards. 'There are exactly three.'

'Well, if you've got that many people looking after you, then the answer is yes, we'd love to come to dinner,' said Hugh.

'What about tomorrow evening?' Kenzo asked.

'Don't you have to consult your diary?' Hugh asked.

'I'm quite sure that the Emperor has no plans or engagements and his sister barely does either. They have become little more than figureheads in this country,' Kenzo explained. 'At least the parliament has seen fit to change the laws, so the young princess will one day become the Empress. We had been very worried that the line was about to come to an end.'

'Oh, I read something about that recently. Of course, it was a terrible tragedy losing her mother like that. And it doesn't sound like the Emperor is likely to remarry?' Hugh replied.

'No. But at least we can look forward to a brighter future for the Imperial family,' Kenzo said.

The door opened and Dolly Oliver entered, followed by Nobu Taguchi from the Ministry.

'Mrs Oliver!' Alice-Miranda ran to greet the woman. 'Your speech was wonderful – but are you feeling all right?'

The old woman nodded. 'Yes, dear. It was just a little warm up there on the stage. But what are you all doing in here?'

'Daddy and Mr Kenzo were friends at school and university. He invited us to have afternoon tea.'

Nobu steered Dolly towards Kenzo, leaving Alice-Miranda to return to her friends, who were still surveying the flawlessly arranged cakes.

Nobu bowed to Kenzo and turned back to Dolly. 'I'd like to introduce the Grand Chamberlain of Japan, Kenzo Aoki.'

Dolly and Kenzo bowed at one another.

'It is a pleasure to meet you, Mrs Oliver, and congratulations on your incredible invention,' said Kenzo.

'Thank you very much,' she replied.

'Hello there, Dolly.' Hugh leaned forward and kissed her on the cheek. 'Well done. But I am a little intrigued about something.'

Dolly intercepted the question. 'Yes, Mr Hugh, I'm sure you are, and I will tell you all about it later.'

Hugh's eyes widened but he gave a discreet nod. 'All right then. Shall I get you some tea?'

Alice-Miranda, Millie and Jacinta enjoyed some of the interesting cakes and tarts on the table while the adults drank tea and talked.

'What's this?' Millie picked up a long stick with several coloured balls nestled along its length.

One of Kenzo's minders was standing beside the table sneaking the odd treat too. He winked at her and said, *'Dango.'*

'I'll give it a go,' Millie said and winked back. She plucked the first pink ball from the end and nibbled. 'It's not too bad. Kind of doughy – like it hasn't been cooked.'

She swallowed the ball and moved onto the green one. As she placed it in her mouth, Millie's face turned a similar shade.

She chewed slowly. Everyone was watching her.

Millie swallowed the food with a huge gulp and mumbled, 'Mmm, delicious.'

The minder grinned. 'She is not a fan of the green tea flavour.'

'No, it's not her favourite,' Jacinta whispered back.

Over Jacinta's shoulder, Alice-Miranda noticed that Mrs Oliver was sitting on her own with a cup of tea. She scurried over, eager to ask a question.

'Oh hello, dear,' the old woman said. 'How's the food?'

'Delicious, but not quite the same as your afternoon teas.' Alice-Miranda plonked herself in the chair beside her. 'I've been wondering . . .'

'Yes?' Dolly met the child's gaze and raised her

eyebrows. 'You've been wondering when I learned Japanese as well as a native speaker?'

Alice-Miranda nodded. 'Yes, exactly.'

'I was planning to tell you and your parents once it was just right,' Dolly began to explain.

'Have you been learning for a long time?' Alice-Miranda asked.

Dolly shook her head.

'That's amazing. I've been learning French for a few years now and I'm still hopeless and my Japanese is just a few words really,' the child babbled. 'Although being here has really helped.'

Dolly set the teacup down on a side table and picked up her handbag from the floor. 'Alice-Miranda, you must promise not to tell anyone about this. Not even your father. I'd like to tell him myself.'

'Of course,' she replied. 'What is it?'

'I've been working on something new.' Dolly opened her handbag and pulled out a small pill case.

'What's that?'

'I've stumbled upon something quite extraordinary,' the old woman said with a grin. 'And I think it could be even more exciting than JAW once I get the formula right.'

Dolly opened the lid and revealed three small compartments, each containing several pills.

Alice-Miranda looked closely. She studied the pictures on each one, then looked back at Mrs Oliver. 'Are they what I think they are?'

Dolly nodded. 'Would you like to speak French or Spanish or Japanese today?' She raised her eyebrows playfully.

Alice-Miranda's jaw dropped and her eyes widened. 'No, it's not possible.'

Dolly nodded. 'Yes, it is. I proved it and that's why Nobu talked about my having perfect Japanese.'

'That explains everything,' Alice-Miranda gasped. 'Except why you didn't want to answer any questions this afternoon.'

'I'm afraid I took a pill yesterday morning and it was working like a charm. I was fluent and I could switch back to English when I needed to. It was all going splendidly and then suddenly when I tried to speak English all that came out was Japanese. It was as if my head was completely scrambled. The effects took hours to wear off and I thought I was going to have to hide in my room for the rest of the conference.'

Alice-Miranda grinned as she imagined Dolly speaking fluent Japanese.

'It wasn't funny at all, I can tell you. I thought I was going to be speaking Japanese for the rest of my days. I don't think Shilly would appreciate that at all.'

'Are you going to try another pill while you're here?' Alice-Miranda asked.

'No, dear. They're going to stay safely away until I get home and run some more tests.' She tucked the pill case deep into her bag.

'How does it work?' Alice-Miranda asked.

'It's very complicated and I'm not entirely sure. I'd always thought it would be a wonderful thing to invent, but when I started fiddling around, I never imagined that it would work.'

'It sounds like something a computer could do, not a pill,' Alice-Miranda said.

Dolly nodded. 'I agree. I was as shocked as you are when I started speaking fluent Japanese down in the laboratory.'

'It sounds like great fun to me,' Alice-Miranda said. 'But don't worry, I promise not to tell.'

Over in the corner, Kenzo checked his watch. 'I'm afraid I must be going,' he told Hugh. 'Could you write down where you are staying? I will send a limousine for you and your family tomorrow evening at six o'clock. I assume there will be ten of you.'

Hugh thought about it for a moment. 'Yes,

Cee and I, Lawrence and Cha, Ambrosia, Dolly, Lucas and the three girls.' He pulled a business card from his wallet and scribbled the address on the back. 'I'm looking forward to it. Are there any protocols we need to be aware of?'

Kenzo shook his head. 'I promise this will be a very relaxed evening in my private apartments.' He passed Hugh a card with his telephone number on it. 'Please call me if you have any concerns.'

Kenzo shook Hugh's hand then bade farewell to the rest of the group and exited through a side door with his minders close behind.

'Well, can you believe that?' Hugh said as he sat down beside Lawrence.

'Great that you got to catch up with your old schoolfriend.'

'Yes, and that's not all,' Hugh said. 'Listen, everyone, I have a wonderful surprise.'

'What is it, Daddy?' Alice-Miranda leapt up from her spot beside Mrs Oliver and rushed over to stand beside her father.

Millie and Jacinta were busy making sculptures with the leftover *dango* balls on the table. They'd made something resembling a sausage dog and were working on a squirrel with huge eyes.

'We're going out for dinner tomorrow night,' Hugh said.

'We're not going to one of those blowfish restaurants, are we?' Jacinta said cautiously. 'Because I'm too young to die.'

Hugh shook his head. 'No, Jacinta, I doubt there'll be a blowfish in sight. Although, on second thoughts, if anyone could afford their own blowfish chef . . . What do you think about dinner at the Imperial Palace?'

Jacinta's eyes almost popped out of her head. 'What did you say?'

'Jacinta, manners!' her mother scolded. 'Hugh, did you really say that we're going to dinner at the Imperial Palace?' Ambrosia was tingling with excitement at the thought of it.

Hugh nodded. 'I most certainly did. Kenzo asked us to join him – just an informal evening in his private apartments, but I gather he's hoping the Emperor and his family might dine with us too.'

'That's amazing!' Millie gasped.

'What will we wear?' asked Ambrosia. She was remembering the first time she'd met Queen Georgiana on the royal yacht *Octavia*. It was at Lawrence and Charlotte's wedding. On that occasion she'd had a whole army of assistants to help prepare her wardrobe for the trip but now she was completely on her own in the fashion stakes.

'Ambrosia, dear, I really don't think it will matter terribly much,' Mrs Oliver said.

'But of course it will. It's not every day one gets to meet a real live Emperor,' Ambrosia fussed.

'Mummy, stop,' Jacinta ordered.

Ambrosia Headlington-Bear took stock. She was a sensible independent woman, not some easily impressed flibbertigibbet schoolgirl.

'Yes, darling, of course you're right.'

'I can't wait to tell Mummy,' said Alice-Miranda. 'It's so exciting.'

Hugh glanced at the clock on the wall. It was just after half past three. 'What do you say we take a quick visit to the Meiji Shrine? We've been trying to get there since yesterday afternoon. Do you want to join us, Dolly?'

'I have to head back in for the panel in half an hour,' she replied. 'And I suspect I'll be in a bit of trouble if I bunk out of that one.' She glanced around, hoping that Nobu from the Ministry hadn't re-entered the room without her noticing.

Alice-Miranda walked over and tugged on

Dolly's sleeve. 'But how will you know what they're saying?'

'I'll just tell Nobu that I would prefer to speak English and use a translator this afternoon. I'm sure he'll understand that I haven't been feeling well.'

The group bade farewell to Dolly, and Hugh told her they'd pick her up on the way to the palace the following evening. She would still be at the conference for another couple of days yet.

'And I can't wait until you come and stay with us,' said Alice-Miranda. 'The futons are much more comfortable than you think.' She gave the woman a tight squeeze.

'What was that for, young lady?' Dolly asked, leaning down to look Alice-Miranda in the eye.

'Just because I miss you.' She grinned and pecked Dolly's powdered cheek.

'And I miss you too, darling girl.'

✴

During their visit to the Meiji Shrine that afternoon, Alice-Miranda, Millie, Jacinta and Lucas wrote wishes on little pieces of paper and tied them to the prayer wall, before watching Japanese men and women, young and old, toss some yen into the offering box near an enormous *taiko* drum. The children were entranced to see the people bow twice, clap twice and bow once more as they made their gift. Lawrence gave the children some money so they could do the same.

Unfortunately, just as Lucas was making his contribution, a young woman recognised Lawrence. Up until then he had been enjoying his anonymity. By the time they went to leave, a small crowd had surrounded the poor man. The admirers asked for photographs and presented pieces of paper for autographs. Fortunately there was a policeman in the area who was also a fan. On noticing the building hysteria, he called for two patrol cars to take the family back to the inn.

'Thank you very much for that,' Hugh said as the cars pulled up outside the *ryokan*.

'It is a pleasure,' the policeman said, getting out of the car to open the back door for Alice-Miranda and the girls. He looked at Hugh sheepishly. 'Do you think I could have a picture with Mr Ridley?'

'Yes, of course. I'm sure he won't mind at all,' Hugh said. Lawrence was in the car behind them.

As the girls got out, Alice-Miranda noticed

another black van parked outside the house on the other side of the alley. Millie saw it too.

'Look at that,' Jacinta gasped as she got out. 'There's another body.'

Sure enough, a gurney was being wheeled out the front door.

'Come on girls, hurry up,' Ambrosia called.

The children exchanged curious looks.

'There's something weird going on over there,' said Jacinta.

Chapter 25

Yuki sniffed and yawned loudly.

'Sorry – am I keeping you up?' Yamato turned and looked at his partner from the driver's seat.

They'd spent the morning glued to the screen in the basement, encountering the same difficulties as the day before with the signal fading in and out more times than they cared to count.

Hatsuko had appeared just after midday, handed them a set of car keys and told them to find Kiko, no matter what.

It was proving far easier said than done. The busy city traffic frequently brought the car to a halt. The screen in the centre of the dashboard had blipped and blinked and just when they thought they were getting close, it disappeared for an hour, springing back to life miles away. They'd been to Shinjuku, then to the Meiji Shrine, and now they found themselves trawling the back streets of Asakusa.

Yamato guided the vehicle into the narrow street. The blip on the screen grew stronger.

'Aha, she is here somewhere, for sure,' said Yuki, nodding. 'Once we find her, we will not let her out of our sight. Then tonight we will take care of things.'

Yamato pointed. 'The signal's coming from that inn.' He stopped the car and took out a small pair of binoculars.

'How can she be staying in an inn? She has no money,' Yuki scoffed.

'Perhaps she has been taken in by a kind citizen?' Yamato suggested.

'Is there somewhere else we can park?' Yuki asked. The roads in Asakusa were narrow and their presence at the front of the inn would no doubt bring unwanted attention. 'What about the alleyway?'

Yamato glanced across and saw what looked to be a dead end. He nodded.

Yuki's stomach let out a strangled whine.

Yamato stared at him.

'What? I'm not allowed to be hungry? My stomach is so empty the sides are touching together.'

Yamato was starving too. 'Then you'd better go and find us something to eat. I'll stay here and keep watch. At least it will be getting dark soon.'

✱

'I'm not being ridiculous. Since when do two people die in the same house on the same day?' Jacinta said dramatically. The girls were sitting on the floor in their room and discussing the strange events of the day.

'I don't know. I'm sure it was just an unfortunate coincidence,' said Alice-Miranda. Privately she thought that two bodies coming out of the same house on the same day was unfortunate indeed. But she was sure there had to be a perfectly sensible explanation. 'When we were there this morning, I noticed a lot of elderly people in the back hallway. Maybe it's an old people's home.'

'Well, I say they're up to something,' Jacinta insisted. 'That man tried to frame me for theft and now bodies are being carted out of their house left, right and centre.'

'I should have taken some pictures so we had evidence,' Millie said with a grin. She was sitting on the floor flicking through the photographs she'd taken since they arrived. 'That's a good one.' She leaned over and showed the girls a picture of the afternoon tea banquet with Jacinta pulling a face at the cakes.

'No, it's not, it's awful!' Jacinta tried to snatch the camera away. 'I'm deleting that.'

'No, you're not,' Millie growled. 'It's my camera and I'll keep whatever I want to.'

Alice-Miranda was absent-mindedly rubbing her finger over the front of her pendant and thinking about the secret Mrs Oliver had shared, when she felt something slightly rough. She pinched the chrysanthemum and, much to her surprise, the front sprang open.

'Goodness!' she exclaimed.

'What's the matter?' Millie asked.

'My pendant is a locket.' Alice-Miranda held it out for Millie and Jacinta to see. She tilted it to see inside. 'And there's a photograph.'

Alice-Miranda undid the clasp and took the locket from around her neck. She stared at the picture of an exquisite young woman. 'She's beautiful.'

'She sure is,' Millie agreed. 'I wonder *who* she is.'

'I don't know, but I'd love to find out,' said Alice-Miranda.

'Maybe you should see if there's any writing on the back of the photo,' Jacinta suggested. 'But I suppose it would be in Japanese, so it wouldn't do you much good.'

Alice-Miranda didn't want to take the picture out. It looked fragile and she hated the thought of damaging it. 'Perhaps Daddy can take me back to where he bought it and we can ask them if they know anything about it.'

'That's the best plan,' Jacinta agreed. 'I'm going to get changed for dinner.' She walked to the wardrobe and pulled out a pretty white dress. She had it on in no time and began to brush her long blonde hair.

'Aren't we staying here again tonight?' Millie asked as she jumped up and ran to the bathroom.

'I think so,' Alice-Miranda said. She was still looking at her locket and thinking about the young woman inside.

There was a knock on the door. Jacinta put down her brush and answered it.

'Oh, hello,' the girl said dreamily.

'You look nice,' the boy said quietly.

Jacinta's heart fluttered and she smiled.

'Is that your boyfriend?' Millie called from the bathroom.

Jacinta turned her head and yelled, 'No, it's Lucas.'

'Yeah, your boyfriend. I could tell because your voice went all weird,' Millie called back.

'It did not,' Jacinta said.

Alice-Miranda ran to the door. 'Hi Lucas. What are you doing?'

'Dad said to meet us for dinner in five minutes.'

'I'm ready now,' Jacinta said. 'Do you want to go downstairs?'

'I'll come too,' said Alice-Miranda, and raced off to grab a cardigan.

'It's okay, you don't have to hurry, little cousin,' Lucas said. 'Why don't you wait for Millie?'

'Yeah, didn't you want to go and ask your father about your necklace?' Jacinta added.

Alice-Miranda nodded. Jacinta and Lucas disappeared, leaving her standing on her own.

'Something strange just happened,' she said as Millie came out of the bathroom.

'What?' the flame-haired child asked.

'Jacinta and Lucas got rid of me,' Alice-Miranda replied.

'What do you mean they got rid of you?' Millie asked.

'They told me I should wait for you even though I was ready to go,' Alice-Miranda said.

Millie nodded. 'You know, I thought he'd started to look at her differently. Before when she used to moon all over him, he'd turn the colour of a beetroot and look as if he was ready to take out a restraining order, but lately he looks quite pleased with himself.'

Alice-Miranda giggled. 'I think it's adorable.'

'Really? Imagine if they get married one day. Jacinta would be your cousin-in-law,' Millie said. 'That would be terrifying.'

Alice-Miranda gave Millie a gentle shove. 'I think it would be lovely.'

★

The family and friends were seated together on a long lacquered table in the dining room. Hugh and

Cecelia had decided that the girls should have a quiet night after their busy day and Charlotte said she was exhausted and wasn't going to go out anyway, regardless of what the others decided.

'I think we might explore a bit more of Asakusa tomorrow morning, girls,' Hugh said over dinner. 'And maybe we can go to the National Gardens after lunch.'

'That's a good idea,' Alice-Miranda agreed. 'Perhaps we could go back to the market and see about my necklace.'

'What about your necklace, darling?' her father asked.

'I was fiddling with it earlier and I discovered that it's a locket.' Alice-Miranda got up to show Hugh. She squeezed the pendant as she'd done earlier and the front sprang open.

'That's a lovely surprise,' her father said.

Her mother leaned in to have a look. 'What a beautiful woman.'

'Yes, that's what we all said too. Wouldn't it be wonderful to find out who she is,' said Alice-Miranda. 'Maybe the man at the store could tell us.'

Hugh thought for a moment. 'Hmm, I doubt it. He told me that he'd only just purchased the locket that morning and I suspect he may not have realised it had hidden treasure. I don't know if I want to go back and ask him. He might want to charge me more – or take it back.'

Alice-Miranda shook her head. 'Oh no, I don't want that to happen. It will just have to be a delicious mystery.'

Charlotte smiled at her niece. 'That's a lovely way to look at it.'

Alice-Miranda knelt down beside Charlotte and looked at her bump. 'Do you have any names picked out?'

The woman ran her hand protectively over her growing stomach. 'Mmm, well, Lawrence is quite keen on Peach for a girl and Melon for a boy,' Charlotte said, straight-faced. 'Of course, we'll have to come up with two girls' names and two boys' names just in case.'

Millie's ears had pricked up at this conversation. 'They're fruity,' she said politely. She whispered to Jacinta behind her hand, 'It sounds like they were inspired by the greengrocer section at Kennington's. Don't tell me they've gone all Hollywood. It sounds like those poor kids are going to have names that will haunt them for the rest of their lives.'

Lawrence grinned at her. 'I heard that, Millie. And of course we're going to do everything in our power to make sure that our children are embarrassed by their parents from birth.'

Alice-Miranda looked at her aunt and shook her head. 'I don't believe you.'

'Why, darling? They're perfectly lovely names.'

'Well . . . they're not exactly what I expected. You're just trying to trick us,' Alice-Miranda said.

Lawrence and Charlotte looked at one another and burst out laughing.

'Oh, they're dreadful – and the first thing that came into my head,' Charlotte chuckled.

'But we had you going, didn't we?' said Lawrence.

Millie snorted and Alice-Miranda rolled her eyes.

'As if,' Jacinta said. 'Lucas would disown you two if his little brothers and sisters were called anything that awful.'

'Don't worry, girls. There'll be no Dweezils or Boo Boos on our watch.'

'Thank goodness for that. But just in case you're stuck, we could give you a list,' Millie suggested.

'Thanks, girls. That's a great idea,' Charlotte laughed. 'We have a few that we like, but we'd love some more.'

Tatsu looked up from his work. He was pleased that Obaasan had found the old lady to take the first vacant room so quickly. But now there was a second space to fill. He didn't care how many of them died in a day, as long as the rooms didn't stay empty for long.

That wasn't his only worry. That afternoon, two police cars had pulled up outside the house. His first response was to panic: had the boy Yoshi seen something? Had he told someone? The thought made Tatsu's stomach churn.

Then his screen had shown the nosey tourists from the inn clambering out of the cars. The police had climbed out too, taken some photographs with the tourists, and then left. It was strange indeed, but nothing to do with him, he'd decided.

Now Tatsu wasn't so sure. He'd seen another car pull up outside the house. A black, unmarked vehicle that tried so hard to be discreet, it stood out like a red bean in a bowl of rice. The car had parked at the end of the alley beside the house and not moved since. Tatsu's mind raced. What if the police had sent detectives to spy on him? What if they'd really been taking photographs of his house? Perhaps someone had reported the black vans and their dead cargo to the authorities. But surely the prefecture would send some officials and not the police? It had to be that Yoshi boy – he would get rid of him as soon as he could.

Chapter 26

'Good morning, girls,' Cecelia greeted the trio as they arrived for breakfast the next morning. She and Ambrosia were wearing their yukatas and both women had wet hair pulled back into sleek buns.

'Hello Mummy, good morning, Ambrosia,' said Alice-Miranda. She gave her mother a hug. 'Where are Aunt Charlotte and the boys?'

Cecelia Highton-Smith set her cup back on the table.

'Cha's having a lie-in and the boys have gone to the bath,' her mother replied.

'*Oooh,*' Millie whispered and poked Jacinta. '*Lucas.*'

'What? Oh, that's disgusting,' Jacinta rebuked her, but began to blush just the same.

Her mother raised her eyebrows and the girls and Cecelia giggled.

'Ambrosia and I have been to the bath too,' said Cecelia. 'I wasn't sleeping so I got up early and popped down for a soak. Ambrosia was already there.'

'And it was heavenly,' the woman said.

'Can we go?' Alice-Miranda asked.

'I don't see why not,' Cecelia agreed. 'Why don't you have your breakfast first and then have a soak. Perhaps after that your father might take you for a walk somewhere close by, although he's been talking about a trip to the National Gardens this afternoon. I want you to have a restful day so you can fully appreciate dinner tonight.'

'What are you doing today, Mummy?' the child asked.

'Charlotte and I have an appointment in the city and Ambrosia is coming with us. We're hoping to be back just after lunch.'

'I can't wait until tonight,' Jacinta said. 'What do you think it will be like?'

'Mr Kenzo said that it would be very informal,' Alice-Miranda said.

Cecelia nodded. 'So your father said. I suspect that Japanese Imperial Palace informal could be a little different to what we imagine.'

Millie grinned. 'So you don't think we'll be having a barbecue in the garden?'

Cecelia shook her head. 'No, I don't think so.'

'I'm sorry about that,' Jacinta said. 'I'd love a steak.'

'What should we wear?' Alice-Miranda asked.

'We could wear our Harajuku outfits,' Jacinta said.

Millie pulled a face. 'I am *not* going to the Imperial Palace dressed as a flying squirrel.'

Jacinta giggled. 'I bet they've never had any other flying squirrels come to dinner. It might cheer up the Emperor.'

'As if.' Millie rolled her eyes.

'Your mother and I have just been talking about that,' Ambrosia said, 'and we have a surprise for you, so don't give it another thought.'

'Really? A surprise?' Millie's eyes widened. 'What is it?'

'A surprise, Millie,' Cecelia said with a wink.

The girl's mouth drooped with feigned disappointment.

'Sorry, Millie, it won't matter how much you pout,' Alice-Miranda told her friend. 'Unlike Daddy, who can't keep a secret to save his life, Mummy is like a steel trap.'

'It's all right,' Millie said, grinning. 'I was just teasing. I love surprises.'

The girls sat down next to Cecelia and Ambrosia, who soon disappeared upstairs to get dressed.

✳

After breakfast, the girls made their way down the hallway towards the bathhouse. Alice-Miranda's father, Lawrence and Lucas were just exiting the men's bath as the girls arrived.

Hugh grinned at his daughter. 'Hello darling.'

'Good morning, Daddy, did you enjoy your bath?'

'Oh, yes. It was very relaxing.'

Lucas's face was red and Millie wondered if he was embarrassed that the girls would know that he and his uncle and father had all been in the bath together. She'd never been skinny-dipping with her parents either. Alice-Miranda noticed the boy's colour too. 'Are you all right?'

'Yeah, fine,' Lucas replied.

'You just look so . . . pink,' Millie said.

'We'll see what colour you are when you get out, Millie.' Lawrence grinned at the girl with her flaming red hair and freckles.

'Why do you say that?' she asked. Millie wondered if the water had some sort of colouring in it.

'Because the water's about a hundred degrees,' Lucas said.

'As if,' Millie scoffed. 'You wouldn't be able to get in at all.'

'You'll see,' Lucas replied. 'Besides, I thought you were the resident authority on all things Japanese. Didn't you read the bath section in your guidebook?'

Millie shrugged. 'I skimmed that part. We have baths at home all the time.'

'Not like this,' Lucas grinned.

'Daddy, can we go for a walk later?' said Alice-Miranda. 'Aki said that there's a park around the corner.'

'I'm sure we can manage it,' Hugh replied. 'Enjoy your bath, girls. We'll see you upstairs in a little while.' Hugh walked off down the corridor with Lucas and Lawrence behind him.

Jacinta set off ahead of the other two girls. She was just about to go through a long blue curtain when Lucas turned.

'Jacinta, that's the men's. The women's is further along.'

'Oops.' Jacinta put her hand to her mouth. 'Thanks. That would have been embarrassing.'

'Yeah, especially if you saw the guy in the bath. Dad and I reckon he's a sumo wrestler.'

Millie giggled.

The girls went a few paces further and parted a long red curtain. They found themselves in a small vestibule, which was empty apart from a single chair and a delicate *ikebana* arrangement on a low table. Another doorway led through to a dressing-room.

'I think that's the undressing-room,' Millie said with a grin as she and the girls walked through. There was a wall of pigeonholes with a white towel perfectly folded in each one.

'Mummy said that you have to put your clothes in the pigeonhole and take a towel,' Alice-Miranda explained.

Millie pulled out the white cloth. It was barely

larger than a face washer. 'I know a lot of Japanese people are small but what's this supposed to cover?'

'Someone must have put a handtowel in there by mistake.' Jacinta pulled a towel from the compartment beside Millie's. It was the same size.

Alice-Miranda pulled out a third towel. It was no bigger than the first two. 'It looks like this is the only size we get.'

'What are we supposed to do now?' Jacinta looked around the room, wishing that Millie had read up on bathhouse etiquette.

'I gather we get undressed,' said Millie. She slipped off her robe and underwear and shoved them into the pigeonhole. She took her towel and walked through another set of curtains.

'Is anyone in there?' Jacinta whispered.

Millie poked her head back through the drapes. 'No, I think we've got the whole place to ourselves.'

Jacinta breathed a sigh of relief and followed Alice-Miranda into a large shower room. White plastic stools and handheld shower nozzles were dotted around the tiled walls. The girls spotted signs indicating that guests should sit and clean themselves thoroughly before getting into the baths, and keep their towels out of the bath water.

Millie pulled up a stool, crossed her legs and grabbed the shower nozzle off the wall. 'This is strangely comfortable, you know,' she said, smiling.

The trio spent five minutes scrubbing and soaping before rinsing themselves off and heading to the adjacent room, where the bath was located. It wasn't like any bath the girls had ever experienced before. At least four metres long and two metres wide, it was more like a small swimming pool. On the far side, a torrent of water cascaded from a ledge, creating a waterfall effect. The steam on the surface looked like fog and Millie remembered Lucas's warning about the temperature.

'I'm going in.' Alice-Miranda plunged her toe into the water and immediately pulled it out again. 'Ow!'

'Is it really that hot?' Millie leaned over and put her hand into the water. She pulled it out quickly too. 'How are we supposed to get in there?'

'Come on, it can't be that bad.' Jacinta dipped her foot in. She stood there for as long as she could bear it and then leapt out, hopping around. 'That's ridiculous. How does anyone ever get in?'

'You've probably just got to sink slowly and allow your body to get used to it,' Alice-Miranda suggested.

The three girls spent the next few minutes dipping their toes before eventually Alice-Miranda plunged into the hot water. Jacinta and Millie got in soon after and the three girls bobbed around like corks.

'This water feels weird,' Millie said.

'I think it's the mineral salts,' Alice-Miranda explained. 'Mummy said that this was an *onsen* and the baths are only called that when they're fed by a mineral spring.'

'Well, I don't care what it's called. It's soo relaxing.' Jacinta swam over to sit on the ledge with the water tumbling onto her shoulders. 'It's like having a built-in masseuse.'

'Since when have you ever had a massage?' Millie asked, paddling over to sit next to her. She let the water crash over her head, plastering her red curls to the side of her face.

'I haven't but this is what I imagine it would be like.' Jacinta wrinkled her nose and sent a splash in Millie's direction.

The girls soaked for ages before Alice-Miranda held her hands out of the water and studied the deep wrinkles crisscrossing her palms like a bumpy road map. 'I might get out. I'm turning into a prune.'

At that moment, the sound of voices floated in from the entrance vestibule.

Jacinta's ears pricked up. 'That's enough for me too.' She swam to the other side of the bath and scrambled out.

'Me three,' Millie said, following her. Although she was enjoying the bath and was quite okay with her friends' nakedness, the thought of sharing the pool with strangers was another thing altogether.

The girls towelled themselves off as best they could then headed back through the shower room and into the dressing area.

'Oh hello,' Alice-Miranda said to the two women who were in various states of undress. The child quickly pulled her *yukata* from the pigeonhole and slipped her underwear on beneath it.

The ladies smiled and nodded. *'Ohayou.'*

Millie and Jacinta were dressed in a flash.

'It's lovely in there but watch out for the water. It's boiling,' Jacinta said as the girls went to leave.

The two young women giggled.

Millie shook her head. 'Seriously? You needed to tell them that?'

'Well it was, wasn't it?' Jacinta frowned.

'I'm pretty sure they're Japanese,' Millie replied.

'They've probably been in a million baths and all of them just as hot.'

'Oh, they must have thought I was an idiot,' Jacinta said, rolling her eyes at herself.

'I disagree,' said Alice-Miranda. 'I'm sure they thought you were kind, that's all.'

'You're so naive, Alice-Miranda,' Millie chided. 'But that's why we love you.'

The girls dashed upstairs to get dressed.

Chapter 27

Half an hour later, the girls, Lucas, Hugh and Lawrence were ready to go to the park that Aki had told them about the day before.

'Do you want us to check and make sure there are no photographers outside?' Millie asked. She was worried that one of the policemen who drove them home the day before might have spilled the beans.

Lawrence looked at Hugh. 'I think we should be okay, but just to be on the safe side, off you go.'

'Don't worry, Lawrence, I could be a private detective in my spare time,' Millie said.

Jacinta snorted. 'Since when?'

'Well, who found Mr Parker and solved the mystery of Mayor Wiley and his dastardly plans for the gold mine last term?' Millie challenged her.

'Alice-Miranda, of course,' Jacinta replied.

'That's not true, Jacinta. Millie and I worked together,' the tiny child said.

'See?' Millie poked out her tongue.

The kids waved goodbye to Aki, found their shoes in the front hall and tumbled out onto the street.

'Are you sure there won't be any photographers lying in wait?' Hugh asked his brother-in-law. He didn't like the idea of sending the children outside to face them on their own.

Lawrence nodded. 'Japan doesn't have much of a paparazzi. Anyway, one call to the police and they'll be gone, so there's no need to worry. Let the kids think they're on the hunt.'

'You take the alley, Alice-Miranda,' said Lucas, 'and I'll head up that way a little and make sure there are no long lenses hiding anywhere.'

'I'll come with you,' Jacinta smiled at the boy.

'Yeah, okay,' Lucas said.

'I'm going with Alice-Miranda,' Millie said, 'because she and I are an awesome team.' She made a monster face at Jacinta.

Lucas and Jacinta walked off in the opposite direction.

'I think a month's holiday with Jacinta is about four weeks too long,' Millie grouched. 'She's really getting on my nerves and it's so obvious that she thinks Lucas is her boyfriend.'

'Just ignore her, Millie. You know she doesn't really mean it,' Alice-Miranda said soothingly.

'Well, if she doesn't mean it, then she shouldn't say it.'

Although the three girls had enjoyed a wonderful time at the beach, Alice-Miranda could sense that, just occasionally, Millie and Jacinta needed a break from one another. While Jacinta had come a long way since her days as the school's second-best tantrum thrower, she still had a prickly temper, which she liked to take out on Millie.

Alice-Miranda spotted a black sedan tucked in the end of the alleyway. It was facing towards them. 'Oh, that doesn't look promising,' she said.

Millie peered down the alley too. 'Do you think we should have a look?'

Alice-Miranda nodded.

The two girls walked towards the vehicle. The dark glass prevented them seeing any of the interior from this distance. But if they had been able to see inside, they'd have discovered a man in a black suit facing a small computer screen. The man's eyelids drooped and his head jerked back as he tried to keep himself awake. His partner was taking altogether too long to fetch coffee after a long night of surveillance. On the screen, a red dot was flashing madly.

Chapter 28

Millie stopped about five metres away from the car. 'Do you really think that could be the paparazzi? It could be anyone. Maybe we shouldn't get too close.'

Alice-Miranda was about to answer when a door opened to her left. It was a side entrance to the house Ambrosia had barged into the day before. Millie grabbed Alice-Miranda's arm, wondering if the pock-faced tyrant from the Itoshii Squirrel store was about to confront them, but it wasn't him or his chubby son.

Another boy stepped into the alley.

'*Ohayou gozaimasu,*' Alice-Miranda said. She looked at the boy. 'Haven't we met before?'

He glanced up at her and shrugged.

'Yes, you gave us directions to the kimono maker yesterday. Thank you ever so much. We made it in time and the kimonos were exquisite. I don't think I've ever seen fabric quite so beautiful before,' Alice-Miranda prattled. 'You're Yoshi, aren't you?'

'*Hai.* I must get to the market,' the child said softly.

'Oh, of course,' Alice-Miranda replied. 'Do you live here?'

'*Hai.*'

'Do you know who owns that?' Millie pointed to the black car.

Kiko glanced up and shook her head. But as she turned to go, she spotted him. One of her aunt's men, unmistakable in his trademark black suit. He'd just turned the corner into the alleyway and was heading towards them.

Alice-Miranda noticed the colour drain from the boy's face. 'Are you all right?'

Kiko gulped. She had to get back inside before he saw her.

Yamato glanced over at the children standing in a huddle. He didn't care much for tourists – they were rude and there were far too many of them.

'I don't feel well,' whispered the boy. He spun around, opened the door and raced back inside. Alice-Miranda went after him.

'What are you doing?' Millie called.

Alice-Miranda turned back, holding the door open. 'I just want to make sure he's all right. He looked as if he might faint.'

'But the Itoshii Squirrel man and that screechy old woman live there.'

'Her name is Obaasan and I'm sure that she wouldn't mind me checking that Yoshi is okay.'

'I'm not going in there.' Millie shook her head. There was no way she wanted to meet either of those people again.

'Well, wait here. I won't be long,' Alice-Miranda said as she closed the door, quickly removed her shoes and located a pair of slippers.

Millie wondered where Lucas and Jacinta had got to. She turned back to face the alley and saw a tall man in a dark suit walking towards the car. He was carrying two takeaway coffee cups.

He glared at her as he walked past. If he was a

paparazzo, he was very well dressed, Millie thought to herself. He put the cups on the roof of the car and opened the passenger door.

A gruff voice emanated from inside the vehicle. Whoever it was didn't seem too happy with the man in the suit.

Millie watched as the driver's door swung open and another man, identically dressed, got out. He reached across the roof of the car and took one of the coffee cups, then walked around the vehicle, stretching his legs and groaning a lot.

Lucas appeared from around the corner and called, 'Millie, is it all clear?'

'I think so,' Millie answered.

'Where's Alice-Miranda?'

'She'll be back in a minute.' Millie wasn't keen to have Hugh and Lawrence cause another scene like Ambrosia had the day before. 'Why don't you and Jacinta go with Hugh and Lawrence and we'll meet you there in a few minutes. I forgot my camera and it would be great to get some pictures of everyone.'

'Do you know where the park is?' Lucas asked.

'Yes, Aki said that it's the first road to the left and then it's just a little way along on the right.'

'Okay, but don't be long.'

Millie stood on the doorstep wondering what to do. The two men were drinking their coffee and talking. Since they weren't watching her, she stood on tiptoes and tried to see inside the window beside the door of the strange house.

Meanwhile, Alice-Miranda had found the boy in a small bedroom just inside the entrance. He was standing in the middle of the room, facing the wall.

'Are you all right?' Alice-Miranda asked. 'I'm sorry about barging in – I just wanted to be sure that you weren't going to faint.'

Kiko nodded without turning around. 'I'm fine.'

'Are you sure?' Alice-Miranda thought the boy looked as if he was struggling to catch his breath.

'*Hai,*' Kiko said. Her mind was racing. They had found her. And now she needed to leave as soon as possible, with or without her mother's diary.

Obaasan's voice echoed down the hall before Alice-Miranda could ask anything more. 'Boy, is that you? I need you to take more tea to Ojiisan. You'd think he would turn green, the amount of tea he drinks. But he is special. My old legs are too sore to get up and down those stairs again today. Hurry up, the squirrel needs my attention.'

When the old man had first arrived, Obaasan had been suspicious. The imperious woman who had arranged his stay gave few details and there was no government pension for him. Each month an envelope full of cash was delivered by a messenger to pay for his room and board. But he was a kind soul and Obaasan had grown to like him.

Kiko flinched, while Alice-Miranda could only guess at what the old woman's tirade in Japanese meant.

Finally Kiko turned around. 'You should go,' she said in English. Her eyes shot to Alice-Miranda's neck. Sure enough, her necklace was there. How she would love to snatch it away, but that would be wrong. The girl's father had paid for it in the market.

'Can I help you? It sounds like Obaasan is cross,' said Alice-Miranda.

Kiko walked past her into the front hall and then through the kitchen door. A tray containing a teapot and cup and a small plate of biscuits sat on the bench. Alice-Miranda followed her.

'That looks heavy,' Alice-Miranda said as she watched Kiko pick it up.

'I'm fine,' Kiko protested. 'Please go, before Obaasan sees you.'

'I'm sure she won't mind if I help you. I met her yesterday, actually. She was a little annoyed about my friend Jacinta's mother barging into the house, but I think she had other things on her mind. We'd just seen someone being taken away from the house in a black van.'

Kiko nodded but said nothing. She had wondered about the commotion yesterday but hadn't dared to ask. As she went to push open the kitchen door, the teapot almost slid off the side of the tray and she just managed to steady herself.

'See, you could do with some help.' Alice-Miranda held the door open and the other child walked through.

'Really, I can take it,' Kiko insisted. Alice-Miranda took the plate of biscuits to lighten the load.

'We saw another black car here yesterday afternoon,' Alice-Miranda commented.

Kiko nodded.

'What a terrible thing to have two deaths in the family in one day,' Alice-Miranda said sadly.

'They are not family,' Kiko said. The words were out of her mouth before she had time to think.

'Do you mind me asking what this place is, then?'

Kiko began to ascend the stairs, with Alice-Miranda close behind her. 'Obaasan looks after the old people. They live here and she cares for them.'

'So it's like a retirement home,' Alice-Miranda said. 'Well, that explains a lot. My daddy's family home was transformed into a lovely place for the elderly. But sadly it tends to be their last home. Is Obaasan your grandmother?'

Kiko shook her head. 'She is just a kind lady.'

'And the man with the scarred face?' Alice-Miranda continued.

'He is her son.' Kiko knew she was saying too much. But something about this child and her big brown eyes made Kiko want to talk.

'Have you lived here long?' Alice-Miranda asked.

'Not really,' Kiko whispered. She reached the top of the stairs and continued down the hallway to the end. She was about to put the tray on the ground to knock when Alice-Miranda leaned forward and did it for her.

'Ojiisan, I have your tea,' Kiko called through the closed door.

Alice-Miranda slid the door open and Kiko walked into the room. Alice-Miranda followed.

An old man with a fuzz of grey hair sat in a chair staring out the window into the alley.

Kiko placed the tray down and set about pouring his tea.

Alice-Miranda watched the graceful way in which Yoshi went about this task.

'*Ohayou gozaimasu,*' said Alice-Miranda. She placed the plate of biscuits on the table beside the old man. His brown eyes stared straight ahead and Alice-Miranda wondered if he was blind. Suddenly he looked up, as if startled back to life.

'Another new helper?' he asked in English.

'Oh no, my name is Alice-Miranda Highton-Smith-Kennington-Jones and it's a pleasure to meet you, sir.' She held out her hand. The old man took it and gave a gentle shake. 'Yoshi wasn't feeling well so I helped him bring the tea up, but I really must be going or Millie will be wondering where I am.'

His eyes came to rest on her locket. 'Where did you get that?' he asked, pointing at Alice-Miranda's neck.

'Isn't it lovely? My father bought it for me at the local market. He bought a paper crane for Jacinta and a cherry blossom for Millie. But I think this is quite special. It's actually a locket and there's a photograph inside. The young woman is lovely but I don't know who she is. Would you like to see her?' Alice-Miranda pressed the locket gently between her fingers.

Kiko gave Ojiisan his tea and watched Alice-Miranda as she fiddled with the pendant.

'There's a bit of a trick to it, I'm afraid,' the child said.

Kiko had to stop herself from reaching out and showing her how to release the catch.

'Oh, here it is.' The front sprang open and Alice-Miranda leaned forward to show the photograph to the old man.

Deep lines ran the width of the old man's forehead and the skin around his eyes creased into hundreds of tiny folds. He stared at the picture.

'Do you know her?' Alice-Miranda asked, watching his reaction.

'She is the Empress of Japan,' the man replied. He brushed his hand against his cheek. 'And before that she was my princess,' he whispered.

'My goodness, that's amazing. I knew that the chrysanthemum was a symbol of the royal family but I hadn't put the two together. I wonder who owned the necklace before me. They must have been very fond of her.'

'Are you up there, boy?' Obaasan yelled from the bottom of the stairs. 'Have you been to the market yet? I need my noodles.'

Kiko held her breath. 'We must go and you must leave. Now,' she instructed Alice-Miranda.

'Yoshi, where are you? I need help today. Not tomorrow. Tomorrow I might be dead, like those old people upstairs,' the woman cackled.

Kiko flinched.

'I can let myself out,' Alice-Miranda whispered. 'Really, I know it's just down the stairs and along the hall.'

'Go on, or you will be in trouble, boy.' The old man emphasised the word boy and winked at Kiko. 'Leave the tray. You can come back for it later.'

Kiko closed the door.

'The Empress. Can you tell me about her?' Alice-Miranda asked.

The man sat stony-faced for a moment. He sipped his tea and looked out the window, as if a clouded memory was coming into focus. 'She was so beautiful and clever.'

'Was?' Alice-Miranda said with a frown.

'*Hai.*' He shook his head. 'She is gone.'

'Did you know her?' Alice-Miranda asked.

A smile crept onto the man's face. 'I have not spoken of Kiyomi for so long.'

'What a pretty name,' Alice-Miranda said. 'I'd love to know more. You see, tonight we're going to dinner at the Imperial Palace and of course I don't want to say anything that might upset the Emperor.'

'You are going to the palace?' The old man's voice wavered.

'Yes. My father went to school with the Grand Chamberlain. I can't wait. I hope we get to meet the young princess too.'

'I don't know anything about that. You must go.' The old man's voice became blunt. 'I am tired.'

'Of course. I'm sorry, I didn't mean to upset you,' Alice-Miranda said. She wondered what she had said wrong. Up until a moment ago he had seemed quite happy to talk.

Alice-Miranda pushed the door open. Before she left, she snuck one last glance at the old man. His face was wet with tears. Princess Kiyomi was more than just his sovereign. She was almost certain of that.

Chapter 29

'I was just about to call the police,' Millie gasped as Alice-Miranda finally appeared at the door. 'I thought you'd be coming out on a stretcher too.'

'Sorry, Millie. I helped Yoshi take some tea upstairs to one of the residents.'

'Residents?' Millie asked. 'Is it a hotel?'

Alice-Miranda shook her head. 'No, it's an old people's home.'

'Well, that explains something, I suppose,' Millie

said. 'Come on, we'd better get going or your father will send a search party.'

Millie grabbed Alice-Miranda's hand and the two girls ran across the alley to the inn, then continued to the first street on the left. They easily found the park, which was tucked just behind some buildings not far along at all. It wasn't much more than a dusty block of ground with some ancient-looking play equipment. Hemmed in by a wire fence, there were bench seats dotted around the perimeter.

Hugh met them at the gate. 'Where have you two been? I was just coming to search for you.'

'Sorry, Daddy. We met a friend and he wasn't feeling very well,' Alice-Miranda explained.

His worried expression softened. 'I should have known you'd have made a few friends by now.'

'Hurry up,' Lucas called from where he was sitting at the top of the huge stone slippery dip. 'This thing is amazing.'

'Coming,' Millie called as she bolted towards the monolithic structure in the middle of the barren ground.

Alice-Miranda stayed behind. 'Daddy, what do you know about the Empress?'

'Not a lot, darling. Why?'

'I just met someone who said that the beautiful woman inside my locket is the Empress Kiyomi and that she had died.'

'Fancy that being the Empress in your locket! Sadly it's true about her passing away. Do you remember the details, Lawrence?' Hugh looked at his brother-in-law.

Lawrence frowned. 'I have a vague recollection of an accident but I'm afraid Japanese royalty hasn't been on my radar terribly much.'

Hugh nodded. 'I think it would have been about five or six years ago now. The Emperor loved driving – he always insisted that he should drive himself whenever possible. There was a terrible crash and his wife was killed and his daughter horribly injured. Yes, that's it. And the Emperor has been unwell ever since. I spoke to Kenzo briefly about the Emperor's ill health but we didn't talk about the accident.'

'Oh, that's so sad.' Alice-Miranda wrapped her fingers around her locket.

'I'm glad you reminded me. I must tell everyone not to mention the Empress at dinner. And it might be best if you don't talk about the photograph in your locket either. I wouldn't want to upset the Emperor or his sister if they do happen to join us.'

Alice-Miranda nodded. 'I'm not sure what I'm wearing this evening but I can tuck it away inside.'

'Good idea.'

'What about the young princess, Daddy? How old is she now?'

'I'm not sure. Probably about ten or eleven, I'd say.'

'Will we get to meet her?'

'That's anyone's guess,' her father replied. 'Why don't you go and have some fun now?'

Alice-Miranda gave her father a hug then bolted off into the middle of the dusty yard.

Lucas, Jacinta, Millie and Alice-Miranda had a wonderful time racing down the slippery dip.

'Do you want to go on that?' Jacinta pointed at a round metal platform. 'It's like a merry-go-round I think.'

'Why not? Lucas shouted. 'We can pretend we're in prep again.'

The children spun themselves silly and bounced up and down on two timber seesaws, which sat side by side.

'That was great fun,' Millie beamed. 'I wish I was six again.'

'You're only ten now,' Alice-Miranda giggled.

'And why shouldn't we play on the equipment – last time I looked we were still kids.'

★

Yuki and Yamato finished their coffee standing outside the car. Yamato glanced inside at the screen but didn't notice that the blip had moved beyond the inn.

'We should have taken her last night,' Yamato told his partner. 'Now we will have to wait until dark again.'

'That inn is locked up tight, you imbecile. Imagine if we'd been caught. Hatsuko would have had us for fish food,' Yuki sighed. He was exhausted and his back had seized up from sleeping in the car.

'She will have us for fish food yet if we don't do it tonight. We must find a way to get to her.'

'All right. You stay here and watch. I will go to the inn and have a look around – see if there is a back door I can unlock.' Yuki walked to the end of the alley and disappeared around the corner.

Yamato's stomach grumbled. He wished his partner had brought something to eat. Surely there was a vending machine close by. He walked to the end of the alley and turned right. He would be back before his partner realised he had gone.

Yuki entered the inn, swapped his shoes for slippers and walked into reception.

The pretty young woman behind the reception desk smiled. *'Ohayou gozaimasu.'*

'Ohayou gozaimasu.'

The man looked anxious.

'Do you have a reservation?' Aki asked cautiously.

'No,' he replied, 'but I would like to look at your facilities and some rooms. I'm thinking of staying here with my family, uh, next time I am in the city. But my wife insists that I inspect the rooms before she will come.'

Aki grinned. 'Of course. This way.' She walked out from behind the counter and indicated for the man to follow her.

'This is the restaurant.' She pointed at the room off to the left of the corridor. 'And we have a very comfortable sitting room where our guests can relax.'

'Very nice.' His eyes darted about. There was no sign of Kiko. 'This is all lovely, but I would like to see some of the rooms and perhaps the bathhouse.'

'I'm afraid that all of our rooms are currently occupied.'

'Surely you understand that I need to see one of the rooms before I will bring my family here,' the man insisted. He looked around and frowned slightly. 'Can you hear that telephone ringing?'

The young woman shook her head. 'No, our telephone is very loud.'

Yuki was losing patience. He needed to have a proper look around – not just for evidence of Kiko, but for another entrance point.

'I can assure you that our rooms are of a very high standard. I can show you some photographs if that would help.'

Yuki shook his head. 'No, that is not good enough. My wife is very particular. She will not come if I cannot confirm that I have seen the rooms myself.'

Aki bit her lip. Perhaps there was one room. Alice-Miranda and her friends were surprisingly tidy for three young girls. Surely she could be in and out in just a few minutes.

'How long were you planning to stay?' Aki asked. If it was only one night it was hardly worth the risk to take him upstairs, but if he was planning to stay for a whole week, that was another thing altogether.

Yuki read her mind. 'At least two weeks.'

'Two weeks. That is a considerable visit,' Aki sighed. 'I will get some keys.'

Yuki smiled to himself. As soon as she was out of sight he scurried along the back hall and quickly found what he was looking for. There was a door. He turned the lock and pushed it open. It led to another alley, which he guessed was at the back of the building. That's how he would get inside tonight. He pulled the door shut and left it unlocked.

He heard the girl's voice. '*Sumimasen*. I have a key.'

Yuki darted back towards the stairs, where she was waiting.

'I had to use the toilet,' he said.

Aki frowned. The toilet was on the other side of the hall. She indicated for him to follow her upstairs.

Back in the car, Yamato had returned with a packet of chips and two bars of chocolate. He settled into the driver's seat and opened the chips before glancing at the blip on the screen.

'What's this?' He focused on the pulsating red dot. It was making small movements around an area a block away from the inn. He wondered if Yuki was following the girl. Surely he must have seen her.

Yamato was certain she had been inside when his partner went to the inn.

Yamato took the telephone from his pocket and dialled Yuki's number. He almost leapt through the roof when the phone started ringing in the car.

He looked down and saw it sitting on the floor under the driver's seat.

'Idiot!'

Yamato wondered if he should risk getting out of the car and taking a look himself. She was still in the same spot. Perhaps Yuki had her but he didn't know what to do next. He looked at the map again and decided that Kiko must be in the little park around the corner from the inn. He would go and find her himself. Hopefully Yuki already had her in his sights.

Chapter 30

'Are you lot hungry?' Hugh called to the children, who were racing about the park playing tag.

'A little bit,' Alice-Miranda called back.

'Let's go and get something to eat then.'

'Okay,' the children agreed, and ran to the bench where Hugh and Lawrence were sitting.

'What do you feel like for lunch?' Lawrence asked them. 'Your father and I were thinking sushi.'

Alice-Miranda nodded. 'Sounds good.'

Lawrence noticed Jacinta's mouth drop. 'Oh

Jacinta, there is nothing better than fresh raw salmon. It melts in your mouth.'

'It can melt in yours but it won't be going anywhere near mine,' she said, shuddering.

'You know, I had some when I was in LA with Dad and it's actually pretty good,' said Lucas.

'Really? You're not just saying that so you can watch me making faces, are you?' Jacinta asked.

'No, of course not,' Lucas said, smiling. 'You know I wouldn't do that to you.'

Jacinta grinned back. 'Maybe I will try it. Just a little bit.'

Lucas winked and Jacinta's cheeks turned pink.

Millie turned to Alice-Miranda and pretended to put her finger down her throat.

Hugh and Lawrence stood up and the group wandered out of the park.

'I think there's a sushi place towards the end of our road,' Hugh said. 'I spotted it when we were walking back from the railway station.'

Alice-Miranda and Millie walked in front of Jacinta and Lucas, with Hugh and Lawrence bringing up the rear. As they reached the corner near the inn, Alice-Miranda turned and called to her father. 'Daddy, can I run up and get my cardigan?'

'That's fine, darling. We'll wait outside for you.'

'I'll come too,' Millie said. She needed to use the toilet.

The girls dashed through the front door, kicked off their shoes and stuffed their feet into their slippers.

'*Konnichiwa*, Aki,' they called as they ran past the woman at the reception desk. She had her head down and seemed focused on something.

'Oh, you are back sooner than I thought,' Aki said, finally looking up. She sped out from behind the desk, annoyed with herself for allowing the demanding man to stay upstairs when he insisted she find him a brochure about the inn.

The girls bounded up the stairs and were almost bowled over by a man in a black suit.

'*Sumimasen,*' Millie apologised. Alice-Miranda did too. The man said nothing, but his dark eyes seemed to drill right through them.

The girls stopped at the top of the landing.

'Wasn't he the man from the alley?' Millie whispered. 'He's creepy.'

They could hear Aki speaking with him downstairs in the hall. They couldn't understand any of the conversation but it didn't sound as if he was pleased.

'Are there any spare rooms up here?' Millie asked, looking along the hallway. As far as she could tell, their party occupied everything on this level.

Alice-Miranda mentally ticked off each room. 'I don't think so.'

'Then what's he doing here?' Millie said. 'He must be a pap. We'll have to tell Lawrence and your father and find out how he got in here in the first place.'

'Aki doesn't sound very happy,' said Alice-Miranda. She pulled the key from her pocket, opened their door and rushed over to the cupboard. She grabbed her favourite pink cardigan while Millie ducked into the loo.

'We should ask Aki about that man,' Millie said as the two girls charged back downstairs. But the woman wasn't at the desk.

'Don't worry, Millie. I'm sure there's a perfectly logical explanation,' Alice-Miranda replied, although she wasn't so sure of that herself.

'He might be outside,' Millie said. 'We could ask him what he was doing.' The girls slipped their shoes back on and hurried out onto the street. But there was no sign of the man.

'Daddy, did you see a man in a black suit come out of the inn?' Alice-Miranda asked.

Her father shook his head. 'Sorry, darling. Lawrence and I have been engrossed in the architecture of the house across the street – interesting, isn't it? Why do you ask?'

'We saw two men in the alley earlier. Then we bumped into one of them on the stairs just now, and he was acting a little strangely,' Alice-Miranda said.

'I saw him,' Lucas said. 'Another man rushed around from the alley and the guy you're talking about came out of the inn right at the same time. They headed that way.' He pointed in the direction of the park. 'If they're here to take photos they must have the world's smallest cameras.'

'Anyway, I'm sure they're not paps,' Lucas said. 'They walked straight past Dad.'

Hugh frowned. 'I'll ask Aki if she knows anything when we get back.'

Alice-Miranda nodded. It certainly was a mystery.

Chapter 31

'So what did you find inside?' Yamato hissed at Yuki as they jogged towards the park.

'The girl in charge barely left me alone for a minute. But I located a rear door and it's now unlocked.'

'Where does it lead?' Yamato asked.

'There is another lane behind the inn. It must come from the alley. We will find it if we have to.'

'And the girl?'

'There was a blue backpack in one of the rooms

but I didn't have much time – perhaps it was hers but there are other children too. They must be hiding her,' Yamato said. 'But why would they take her in? She has no money.'

'The necklace! Do you think she could have sold it?' Yuki asked his partner as they jogged around the corner towards the playground.

Yamato shook his head. 'No! Don't be ridiculous. It has a photograph of her mother inside.'

The screams and laughter of children echoed along the street.

Yuki scanned the small patch. 'Is she in there?'

'I can't tell. You take one side and I'll take the other. Try not to arouse suspicion.' Yamato stalked off, taking note of each child. Too small, too fat, too old, too young. As far as he could tell, she wasn't there. And now that he thought about it, he didn't know what they would do if she was. They couldn't snatch her in broad daylight.

Yamato looked up. What on earth was Yuki doing? He'd told the idiot not to arouse suspicion and now he was standing at the bottom of the slippery dip catching the children as they sped through the air at the bottom.

'Whoopee!' he yelled as he snatched hold of a toddler who was about to land on the ground.

The little boy laughed and hiccupped at the same time.

'You poor little fellow.' Yuki set the boy down on his feet.

He didn't see his partner approach. He leapt into the air when Yamato hissed into his ear. The little boy began to cry in big scared sobs. 'Mama, mama,' the child wailed.

A woman hurried over. Yuki glared at his partner and then turned to the woman. 'I'm sorry about my friend. He didn't mean to frighten your little boy, but at least the boy no longer has the hiccups.'

'Stupid!' the woman hissed. She took her little boy's hand and hurried to the other side of the park.

'What are you doing?' Yamato's fingers dug into Yuki's bicep as he guided the man away.

'You didn't need to do that,' Yuki whispered. 'I was just helping the children.'

'You are supposed to be looking for Kiko,' Yamato said. 'She's not here. Let's hope she's gone back to the inn.'

The two men walked past the inn to their car. They hopped inside and stared at the screen. The blip had moved but not far: it was now down the other end of the street.

'How did she get past us?' Yamato asked furiously.

Yuki shrugged. He was tired of this game of cat and mouse and just wanted to go home and sleep.

The telephone rang.

Yuki looked at the number and rolled his eyes.

'Aren't you going to answer it?' Yamato asked.

'And get screamed at again?'

Yamato reached over and snatched the handset. '*Konnichiwa* . . . Yes, we are close.' There was a long pause while Hatsuko's voice hissed through the speaker like a serpent.

'Guests? What guests?' Yamato said.

Yuki's brow creased. Visitors to the palace were few and far between, and even then he and Yamato would know about it months ahead of time.

'Would you like us to come back?' Yamato asked.

The screeching from the other end grew louder.

Yamato winced. '*Hai. Hai.*' He slammed the phone onto the dashboard.

'Well?' Yuki asked.

'We must find her or you and I will be posted to the garbage service.'

Chapter 32

Jacinta not only tried sashimi at lunch but enjoyed it. Once she got past the idea that the fish was raw, she decided it tasted a lot like smoked salmon without the smoking part.

'I can't wait until tonight,' Alice-Miranda said as they left the restaurant. She shivered with excitement. 'I hope we do get to meet the Emperor. I wonder if Aunty Gee knows him.'

'I suspect she does,' Hugh replied. 'There wouldn't be too many royals in the world who Aunty Gee hasn't met.'

Outside, the clear blue sky had been replaced by heaving thunderclouds.

'Looks like we might get wet,' said Lawrence, as a large drop spattered on the footpath in front of him.

'Pity we didn't bring any umbrellas,' Hugh said.

'Never mind, we can make a run for it,' Lawrence replied. 'It's not far.'

The group began their dash down the street.

'It's getting heavier,' Alice-Miranda called.

A lightning bolt slashed the sky and thunder pealed like an ancient bell.

'Oooh, I hate storms,' Jacinta wailed. Lucas slipped his hand into hers and the two of them ran along together.

'I love them,' Millie yelled and twirled around with her head facing up to the sky.

The rain belted down and soon the children, Hugh and Lawrence were soaked to the skin.

Chapter 33

After drying off, the children spent the rest of the afternoon playing board games and chatting in the sitting room downstairs. Aki taught them how to fold origami cranes too, and left the group with a lovely pile of pretty paper squares and instruction sheets for different animals. Millie made a bat, a butterfly and something that should have resembled a cat but looked more like a frog. The storm put paid to Hugh's plans to visit the National Gardens. It lasted for hours and the inn took on an eerie quality in the dim light. Lucas entertained the girls with spooky stories about the old chapel over at Fayle School. The girls giggled at his impersonations of the teachers, especially Mr Lipp and Professor Winterbottom.

Jacinta looked at him dreamily. 'You know, you should be an actor like your father.'

Lucas shrugged. 'I guess it would be kind of fun. But I'd hate to have people staring at me all the time.'

'What, like Jacinta does?' Millie asked.

'I do not,' Jacinta snapped.

'Uh, yeah, you do,' Lucas said, grinning.

'Well, I won't any more,' Jacinta fumed.

'No, it's okay. I don't mind,' said Lucas.

Millie rolled her eyes.

The group was interrupted by Cecelia, who had arrived back a little while earlier and been upstairs arranging outfits for the evening's visit to the palace.

'Hello darlings, time to get ready.'

Alice-Miranda began to pack up the game. 'What do we have to wear?'

'There's a surprise or three in your room,' Cecelia replied.

'What about Lucas?' Jacinta asked.

'I'm afraid it's just a boring old dinner suit for you,' she told her nephew.

Alice-Miranda put the boxes back on the shelf while the others tidied up the cushions and origami paper before they went upstairs.

'Let's see what we have here,' said Cecelia as she slid open the door to the girls' room. Hanging on the wardrobe doors were three beautiful kimonos.

'Oh my goodness, are they for us?' Jacinta asked. She immediately recognised the lilac one as the same gorgeous garment she'd tried on the day before.

'Yes, the kimono makers insisted on sending them for you all as a gift,' Cecelia nodded.

'They're amazing,' Millie gasped.

Ambrosia walked into the room. 'Do you really like them?'

'They're beautiful,' said Alice-Miranda. She rushed over and studied the intricate floral patterns.

'How about we get you into them and then we can have a play around with your hair?' Cecelia suggested.

'What are you wearing, Mummy?' Alice-Miranda asked. 'Do you have a kimono too?'

'No, darling. We wouldn't want to overdo it.'

Ambrosia passed her daughter the lilac kimono

and then handed Alice-Miranda the pink one. Millie's was the most stunning shade of pale green.

Jacinta stroked the silk. 'I love it.'

'Anyone home?' Charlotte asked as she slid open the screen and walked into the room. 'How are my little geisha girls getting on?'

Alice-Miranda spun around. 'You look gorgeous.'

Charlotte was wearing a stunning magenta-coloured empire-line gown, with long sleeves and a scoop neck.

'I feel like a whale,' Charlotte said as she patted her baby bump.

'Well, you don't look like one,' Alice-Miranda said.

'Thank you, sweetheart. I'm just so tired all the time. I can't imagine being even more tired when these guys arrive.'

The girls slipped into their kimonos and Charlotte lined them up to do their hair, while Cecelia and Ambrosia ducked off to get dressed.

Half an hour later, Cecelia reappeared carrying three pairs of *geta* sandals, and little silk purses and hair ribbons to go with the girls' kimonos.

'I love your dress too, Cecelia,' said Millie as she cast her eye over the woman's striking blue gown.

Ambrosia was wearing an equally gorgeous emerald satin evening dress.

'Daddy said that this was an informal evening,' Alice-Miranda said thoughtfully. 'And we're all dressed as if we're off to a ball.'

'Your father telephoned Kenzo and asked what he meant by informal. Kenzo said he'd *just* be wearing his dinner suit, so we took that to mean informal was a step down from top hats and tails.'

'I'm glad Daddy called,' Alice-Miranda said. 'It would have been embarrassing to arrive underdressed.'

'Or undressed,' Millie giggled.

'I couldn't agree more, Millie,' Cecelia said. The woman's diamond earrings caught the light and sparkled as brightly as her smile. She glanced at her watch. 'Oh heavens, it's almost six. We'd better get downstairs.'

Lawrence stepped out of his room, followed by Lucas and Hugh. 'Who are these gorgeous babes?' he asked with a grin. 'I hope they're coming out with us.'

'Oh, Uncle Lawrence,' Alice-Miranda giggled. 'Please behave yourself.'

Chapter 34

Yuki looked up from the newspaper he was reading and stared at the blip on the screen. 'She's on the move.'

Yamato turned the key in the ignition. 'I'm sick of trying to do this on foot. Let's follow her in the car. Besides –' he put the window down and looked skywards – 'it's almost dark and it might rain again.'

He only managed to drive a few metres forward; the road was blocked by an enormous black limousine parked outside the inn.

Yuki cursed and threw his newspaper on the back seat. 'Not again. We can't lose her this time.'

The limousine moved off and the blip did too.

'Can you see her?' Yamato looked left and Yuki scanned the right-hand side of the road.

'No, but she's picking up speed,' said Yuki. He stared at the blip. 'She should be right in front of us.'

'But clearly she is not,' Yamato huffed. 'Stupid system – it doesn't work properly at all.'

The limousine turned right at the end of the road.

Yamato stopped at the traffic lights and watched as the blip sped away from them. The two men looked at the screen and then at each other.

'Is it possible?' Yamato hissed.

'She's in that limousine?' Yuki growled. 'But how? Who's helping her? And where is she going?'

Yamato looked up and planted his foot on the accelerator. The car surged through the intersection, narrowly missing a truck. He slapped his hand on the steering wheel as the traffic ground to a halt in front of them.

He looked at the footpath. It was crowded with people.

'Nooooo . . . You're a maniac!' Yuki protested and squeezed his eyes shut.

Yamato leaned on the horn and people scattered left and right.

'Tell me where the limousine is going,' said Yamato. He was straining to see, but it had melted into the traffic.

Yuki opened his eyes and looked at the blip. It was heading towards Shinjuku.

'There it is.' Yamato pointed at the limousine as it pulled up outside the Royal Plaza Hotel. Yamato stopped on the side of the road and watched.

An old woman with a helmet of brown curls and wearing a sparkling blue evening gown walked out of the hotel foyer. The limousine driver got out and opened the back door. The woman hopped inside and moments later the car took off again.

'What is going on?' Yamato moaned. He followed the car through the traffic.

Yuki shrugged. 'We're heading towards the palace. I do *not* understand.'

Things became even more confusing when the limousine pulled up at the palace gates and was ushered through.

'You must call her,' Yamato said.

'You call her,' Yuki argued. 'I don't want to.'

'Give me that.' Yamato snatched the phone from

his partner and dialled the number. His hands were trembling and his throat was dry. 'I am afraid that I have bad news, Your Majesty.'

✹

'What a lovely night for a party,' said Alice-Miranda as she stared out the window at the city streets.

'It is,' Millie agreed. She ran her tongue over her teeth. 'Oh no, I forgot to brush before we left. Does anyone have a mint?'

'I do, dear.' Dolly flicked open her handbag and foraged about. She dropped a small white pill into Millie's hand.

'May I have one too?' Jacinta asked.

'Of course.' Dolly handed her another.

'I wonder what sort of food we'll have tonight,' Alice-Miranda said.

'Not too weird, I hope,' Jacinta muttered. She swallowed her mint and wondered about its strange taste.

Chapter 35

'Oh, Daddy, the palace is gorgeous,' Alice-Miranda gasped.

The limousine drove through a well-lit garden of ornamental trees and on towards the main building. Its white-washed walls and upturned roofline shone in the darkness.

The car continued around the long driveway and pulled up in a courtyard behind the palace. The group was greeted by Kenzo and a small army of staff, who were lined up outside a set of timber gates.

'Hugh-san.' Kenzo bowed, then shook his friend's hand. 'Thank you so much for coming – and at such short notice.'

'No, thank you. This lot have been buzzing all day,' Hugh grinned. 'I hope it wasn't too much trouble to organise.'

'On the contrary. It is the most exciting thing that has happened here in a very long time.'

Hugh introduced Kenzo to his family and friends. Being the diplomat that he was, Kenzo remembered everyone's names from the day before and had managed to do some research on Cecelia, Charlotte and Ambrosia Headlington-Bear.

'You look magnificent, girls,' he complimented Alice-Miranda, Millie and Jacinta. 'And your mothers and aunt are rare jewels too. And of course, Mrs Oliver, you look smashing. Please, come this way.' He led the party past the staff and through the gates into a long hallway.

Alice-Miranda noticed some of the young women giggling behind their hands as Lawrence walked past.

'What about our shoes?' Millie said quietly.

'It is all right, Miss Millie. You may wear your shoes here – it is considered a public space. You will see that I have plenty of slippers in my apartment.'

'An apartment? That doesn't sound very exciting,' Jacinta whispered behind her hand to Millie. 'I thought we were at a palace.'

About halfway down the hallway, Kenzo turned left into a timber-lined foyer. Two enormous faux dogs guarded the entrance and, sure enough, there were four rows of slippers precisely lined up in an ornate shoe rack.

Kenzo stretched out his arm. 'Please help yourselves.'

The slippers weren't like anything the girls had ever seen before. Beautifully embroidered with gold chrysanthemums across the front, there were pairs to fit every foot size imaginable.

'This way.' The doors opened and Kenzo led the group inside an enormous entrance hall.

Elegant in its simplicity, the room was bounded by *shoji* screens. In the centre was a perfect miniature tree atop a carved stand.

'Is that a bonsai?' Alice-Miranda asked the man.

'*Hai*, it is my hobby,' he replied. 'Do you like it?'

'I love it,' she said as she studied the delicate cherry blossom.

Kenzo bowed and said, '*Arigatou.*' He walked

towards another set of double doors and pushed them open. 'Please join me for drinks before our meal.'

'Whoa!' Jacinta gasped.

The room was the size of a tennis court. There were at least four different lounge areas as well as a grand piano and various other antiquities adorning the space.

'Some apartment,' Millie whispered to the girl.

'I'll say.'

Kenzo clapped his hands and within seconds the room was crowded with staff, offering all manner of drinks and canapés.

A rotund waiter no taller than Lucas walked over to the children. He was holding a tray with a variety of options.

Alice-Miranda smiled at the man. '*Konbanwa. Watashi wa* Alice-Miranda *desu.*'

'You have very good Japanese, miss,' the man complimented her. 'What would you like to drink? I have pink lemonade, mineral water, iced green tea and guava juice.'

Jacinta and Millie both pulled faces at the iced green tea.

'I'd love a lemonade, please.' Alice-Miranda took a tall glass from the tray.

'I'll have the same,' Jacinta said.

'I think I'll try the guava juice,' said Lucas.

'Do you have coffee in a can?' Millie asked.

The man frowned at her.

'You know, like the ones you can get in vending machines?'

'Millie, I don't think they'll have that here,' said Alice-Miranda quietly.

'Oh no, miss. I do have that. I will be back in a moment.' The man scurried off through a doorway at the other end of the room.

'Are you even allowed to drink coffee?' Jacinta asked.

'Every now and then Mum gives me a sip of hers,' Millie said.

'But this is a whole can,' said Alice-Miranda. 'You'd better just have a little bit or you might be awake all night.'

The adults had followed Kenzo to one of the lounge areas, where they were enjoying French champagne or, in Charlotte's case, sparkling mineral water.

'I'm starving,' said Millie. She eyed off a couple of waiters who were walking towards them.

'May I offer you *shishamo*?' the young man said with a grin.

Millie looked at the plate. A row of small fish, complete with tails and googly eyes, stared back at her. 'No, thank you.'

'Miss, they are very tasty,' said the waiter enticingly.

'I'll try it.' Lucas leaned over and picked up one of the fish. 'Here goes.' He downed the whole thing, head and all. The boy's face contorted in all sorts of directions. He swallowed and took a large gulp of juice. 'Mmm . . . delicious.'

'Would you like another, young man? But this is for the heads.' The man pointed at the bowl in the middle of the platter.

'Oh.' Lucas shuddered. 'I couldn't possibly. I'm full.' He shook his head and patted his tummy, then turned away and wiped his tongue on the napkin.

'Not so good, hey?' Millie giggled.

'That was disgusting. I thought I was going to throw up.'

'Well, you did eat the head when you didn't have to,' Millie teased.

Lucas gagged. 'Stop reminding me.'

'Why couldn't we just have a barbecue?' Jacinta moaned. 'I could eat a cow right now.'

The children wandered around the room looking at the array of artefacts and artworks. There were samurai swords and a full suit of armour in one corner, and a display case of the most delicate porcelain figurines. But it was Kenzo's bonsai collection that most fascinated the children.

'Those little trees are amazing.' Jacinta peered into the branches of a perfectly clipped maple. She was half-expecting a miniature squirrel to run down the trunk.

'Look at this one.' Millie pointed at another of the delicate plants. 'It looks like our Christmas tree. Well, a tiny version of it.'

'Do you think the Emperor will come to dinner?' Lucas asked. 'Dad said that he's hardly been seen for ten years.'

'Like Miss Grimm,' Alice-Miranda said.

'Hey, that's true. What a strange coincidence,' said Millie. The waiter had reappeared with her coffee, which he'd poured from the can into a glass. Millie took a sip.

'What's it like?' Jacinta asked.

'Mmm, it's very sweet and it doesn't really taste like coffee. At least, not the sort my mum drinks.' She took another gulp. 'Actually, it's pretty good.'

'Oh no, she's going to be dancing on the tables tonight,' Jacinta teased.

'No, I won't,' Millie shook her head. 'I'd only do that for strong coffee. This must be like the Under Twelves version of coffee in a can.'

At the other end of the room, the double doors opened.

Like a military parade, the staff quickly formed two lines down the centre of the room.

'Ah, Your Majesty, might I say you are looking very beautiful this evening,' Kenzo exclaimed, before giving a low bow.

A woman walked down the lines of attendants. She wore a simple black beaded gown with her hair pulled tightly into a perfect bun.

'We should join the grown-ups,' Alice-Miranda whispered and then scurried with her friends to the other end of the room.

'May I introduce my good friend, Hugh Kennington-Jones?' Kenzo gestured towards Hugh, who bowed as low as his back would allow.

'And of course, you have seen this man before.' Kenzo nodded at Lawrence Ridley.

Hatsuko blushed. 'It is a pleasure to meet you, Mr Ridley.'

'And you, Princess.' Lawrence smiled and Hatsuko reached for Kenzo's arm to steady herself.

'Did you see that?' Jacinta grinned. 'She almost fainted. That happened to me too the first time I met him.'

'It happens to you now,' Millie quipped.

The introductions continued until Kenzo reached Alice-Miranda.

'*Konbanwa*, Your Highness. I'm sorry, but I haven't learned how to say that in Japanese. *Watashi wa* Alice-Miranda *desu*.' The child bowed at right angles. She stood back up and beamed at the woman.

'Never mind,' Hatsuko murmured. She studied the child, a slight sneer creeping onto her lips. She hadn't realised that Kenzo had invited young ones into the palace.

Alice-Miranda didn't notice the change in Hatsuko's expression. 'Your dress is lovely. Will Princess Kiko be joining us?'

Hatsuko smiled thinly. 'No. She is not feeling well.'

Hatsuko had thought her head was going to explode when those two idiots told her that Kiko was at the palace. So far they had searched high and low and there was no sign of the child anywhere. Hatsuko pretended to smooth her hair. In the process, she pressed the earpiece further inside her ear and listened. If Kiko was spotted, Yuki and Yamato were to tell her immediately.

'I am so sorry to hear it,' said Alice-Miranda. 'I would love to meet her.'

'Yes, I'm sure that you would.'

As Kenzo finished the presentations, he nodded towards a young man dressed in a black suit. The fellow walked towards a large gong and picked up the mallet beside it. With great ceremony he hit the centre of the metal disc and the sound reverberated throughout the palace.

'It is time for us to eat,' Kenzo said. He led the party through the far set of double doors and into a dining room. The long mahogany table was laid with exacting precision.

'Extraordinary,' Dolly Oliver mumbled as the group was guided to their seats. It seemed that for each guest there were at least two staff members.

'We'll have to employ a few more people I think, Cee,' said Hugh, arching an eyebrow at his wife. 'Our dinner parties are positively impoverished compared with this.'

'I think our dinner parties are just fine,' Cecelia whispered. 'And this, my darling, is ridiculous.'

Kenzo was seated at the head of the table with Princess Hatsuko to his left. The adults were then seated along each side and finally the children were together at the other end. The chair opposite Kenzo was empty.

'Do you think that's for the Emperor?' Millie whispered to Alice-Miranda.

'Maybe, but I don't think they'd have put all of us together down here if they thought he was going to come. He'd probably prefer some adult company.'

Hatsuko leaned towards Kenzo. 'Did you tell my brother about your guests?' she asked.

'*Hai*. I do not expect him for dinner but he said that perhaps he will feel up to meeting Mr Ridley at the end of the meal.'

Hatsuko rolled her eyes. Her brother hadn't been up to anything for years. She couldn't imagine that the presence of a movie star would change that.

Kenzo spoke to one of the waiters and within seconds the first course was served.

Jacinta stared at what looked like a flower on her plate. It was cream in the centre with pink petals and a touch of green to look like a stem.

The waiter behind her chair leaned forward and whispered, 'It is a potato, miss.'

'A potato? How did they make it look like that?'

'Japanese food is not just for nourishment of the body, miss. It is for enrichment of the soul.'

'Ohhh,' Jacinta nodded. She had no idea what he meant but it sounded impressive.

'I hope there's more than this,' Millie muttered.

A waiter standing behind the girl also leaned forward and murmured, 'Do not worry, miss. This is the first of many courses.'

Millie turned and smiled at him. 'Great. I'm starving.'

Kenzo nodded towards his guests. 'Please, let us eat and enjoy.'

He was just about to take his first mouthful when the doors at the end of the room slid open.

Kenzo looked up. His jaw dropped and he was on his feet in no time. 'Oh, Your Majesty.'

The adults and children took their lead from him too – except Jacinta, who was busily studying the floral potato and wondering how on earth it had been crafted.

Lucas leaned down and whispered in her ear, 'Jacinta, stand up!'

'What?' Jacinta looked up and saw that everyone was on their feet. 'Oh sorry.' She scrambled to stand. 'Why didn't you tell me? Are we having a toast or something? We just sat down.'

Lucas elbowed her gently and pointed towards the doorway.

Kenzo bowed deeply. The rest of the group did too. Jacinta hurriedly joined in.

The man in the doorway merely blinked at the group. His face was drawn and his dinner suit hung loosely from his thin frame.

'I'm glad there'll be lots to eat,' Millie whispered to Alice-Miranda. 'The Emperor looks like he could do with some fattening up.'

At the other end of the table, Hatsuko's stomach lurched. Her brother had not dined with guests for years. She silently cursed Kenzo and his chance meeting with Hugh Kennington-Jones.

'Your Majesty,' Kenzo said and bowed again. Everyone else did too.

The man nodded.

Kenzo smiled. He then walked towards the Emperor and whispered something.

'Ladies and gentleman, I would like to introduce His Imperial Majesty, Emperor Jimmu.'

'*Konbanwa,*' the Emperor said in an unexpect-edly deep voice. 'Please sit down.'

Kenzo looked at the empty chair at the head of the table then glanced at his own seat. 'Would you like to sit beside your sister?'

'That is your place, my friend. I will sit right here.'

Within a second the chair had been pulled out, the perfect place setting straightened and the Emperor was seated.

'I cannot tell you what a thrill it is to have you with us,' Kenzo said quietly.

'It is about time that I live again, my friend.'

Kenzo then went around the table introducing the guests one by one. Alice-Miranda was seated to the Emperor's left.

'This is Mr Hugh and Ms Cecelia's daughter, Miss Alice-Miranda,' Kenzo concluded the intro-ductions.

'It's a pleasure to meet you, Your Majesty.' The child looked up at him with her brown eyes as big as saucers. 'I love your house – well, your palace, of course. It's very beautiful and I imagine that this is only a small part of it.'

'This is Kenzo-san's apartment. But you are

right. This palace is far too big and empty,' said the Emperor sadly.

'Well, it's gorgeous all the same. We have a lovely home too, although it doesn't compare to this. Mummy and Daddy have lots of parties. I think it makes the house feel treasured. Do you like parties?' she asked.

Emperor Jimmu stared blankly. He looked as if he was lost in a happy memory. 'You know, I do, but there have been none for such a long time. Not since my beautiful Kiyomi . . .'

Hatsuko was listening from the other end of the table. She was pleased to hear the dead Empress's name. Surely he would be sucked back into his grief, and he would return to his room to mourn in private, just as he had done for years now.

Alice-Miranda nodded. 'I am sorry about the Empress.'

Kenzo held his breath.

'She was very beautiful. But you have a daughter and I'm sure she must be lovely, like her mother. You must take great comfort knowing that a part of your wife lives on. Not that I know much about anything yet because I'm only eight and one-quarter. I can't imagine how hard it would be.'

The Emperor stared at Alice-Miranda. 'Did you say that you were only eight and one-quarter?'

She nodded.

'Then you are the wisest eight-and-one-quarter-year-old I have ever had the pleasure to meet.' A tear welled in the corner of his eye and he quickly brushed it away.

Hatsuko was waiting for him to run from the room. But he didn't. Instead he looked up at his sister.

'Where is my daughter?' he asked. 'I would like her to join us for dinner.'

'Oh!' Alice-Miranda clasped her hands together. 'That's wonderful, Your Majesty. I've been hoping that we might meet the princess.'

Hatsuko's stomach clenched. She stood up from the table and bowed as she exited the room.

In the hallway she hissed into her watch. 'Where is she, you fools?'

Back inside the dining room, Kenzo beamed. For the first time in years it seemed as if things in the Imperial household were looking up.

Chapter 36

Hatsuko fled along the corridor and down into the secret dungeon, where Yuki was monitoring the screen.

'Well, where is she?' Hatsuko said, and stamped her foot on the floor.

'It is a mystery, Your Majesty. According to this, she is in Kenzo's dining room.'

'In the dining room! She cannot be! I have just come from there and unless Kiko has transformed herself into a small brunette child or a blonde or a redhead, she is not there.'

'May I ask who you are dining with?'

'A friend of Kenzo's from his university days and his family. His name is Hugh Kennington-Jones and his brother-in-law is the actor Lawrence Ridley.'

'Ah, the famous movie star?' Yuki grinned. 'He is a handsome man.'

Hatsuko clopped him over the back of the head. 'I know that, you fool.'

Yuki gulped. He had a vague memory of a brunette and a red-haired child near the inn. 'May I ask what the children look like?'

'Here, look on the computer. Search for them and I am sure there will be pictures, if you are so fascinated.'

Within a minute a photograph of Hugh Kennington-Jones and his wife and daughter appeared on the screen.

Yuki felt as if he'd just swallowed a mouthful of sand. Yamato arrived in the room.

'I've seen that child before,' he said, pointing at the screen.

Yuki nodded. '*Hai*. Where?'

'She was in Harajuku right outside the crêperie and again inside the store where we thought the princess was. She was at the inn we have been watching too.'

Hatsuko drummed her fingers on the desk. 'So do you think she is hiding the princess?'

The two men shrugged.

Hatsuko's eyes widened. 'You numbskulls! The princess has outsmarted both of you!' The woman screeched as she ran from the room and back towards Kenzo's apartment.

She stood outside the door, smoothed her hair and took several deep breaths. Then Hatsuko strode into the room. To her dismay, her brother was giggling like a schoolboy. He and the brunette child seemed to be deep in conversation, but he looked up as she entered.

'Where is Princess Kiko?'

'I am afraid that she is not feeling well. She is sleeping,' Hatsuko lied.

The Emperor frowned and cocked his head. 'I have not seen her for days now.'

Hatsuko wanted to correct him. He hadn't seen his daughter for much longer than that. The last time the child had been summoned to his room, he'd taken one look at her and burst into tears. Hatsuko had spent many months making sure that the child knew it was her fault entirely that he was unwell. She reminded him too much of her dead mother.

'I am sure the princess would love to have met the children, but perhaps next time,' Hatsuko said blandly.

'Oh, I can't imagine that there will be a next time. I mean, it's not every day that one gets to meet the Emperor of Japan,' Alice-Miranda babbled.

The Emperor looked at Hatsuko closely. 'We must see if she is awake and feeling better after we have finished our meal.'

Hatsuko gulped and turned her attention to the children. She needed to work out exactly what the princess's game was and how this perky little brat and her friends were involved. 'Have you enjoyed seeing the city?'

'*Hai*. Tokyo is wonderful,' Alice-Miranda enthused.

'We went to Harajuku and got to dress up,' Millie added.

'And Hugh bought us some beautiful necklaces so that we'll always remember our first visit to Japan,' Jacinta said. 'Would you like to see them?'

Hugh looked at his daughter and frowned. Alice-Miranda gave a tiny nod.

'Mine's a paper crane,' Jacinta pulled the necklace out of her kimono and showed it off.

'And mine's a cherry blossom.' Millie did the same.

'They are both charming and symbolic of our country,' the Emperor said.

'What about you?' Hatsuko stared at Alice-Miranda, her dark eyes narrowing.

The child smiled. 'Oh, mine's a lovely little disc.'

'No, it's a chrysanthemum locket with a picture of a beautiful woman inside,' said Jacinta.

'Really? A locket, you say?' Hatsuko smiled thinly. 'Please show me.'

Hugh looked across the table and nodded. Alice-Miranda could hardly refuse the princess's request. At least the Emperor had spoken openly of his wife and daughter, so it didn't seem like Alice-Miranda's locket would upset him at this point.

Alice-Miranda pulled the necklace from inside her kimono.

'Would you come here so I can see it?' Hatsuko asked.

The child hopped down from her seat and walked to the end of the table. Hatsuko had to stop herself from tearing the necklace from the girl's throat.

'The catch is a bit tricky,' Alice-Miranda said.

Hatsuko pushed her hand away. 'It's fine. I am

very good with jewellery.' She popped open the front of the locket and stared at the photograph. 'She's very pretty.'

'Yes, she is,' said Alice-Miranda.

'May I see?' the Emperor asked.

'Of course,' Hatsuko said.

'Do you think that's a good idea, Princess?' Alice-Miranda whispered to the woman.

Hatsuko eyeballed the child. 'Why wouldn't it be?'

'Please, I would love to see.' The Emperor beckoned Alice-Miranda back to the other end of the table.

He lifted up the pendant and inspected the outside. 'It is a thing of great beauty.' He turned it over and gasped.

'Are you all right, Your Majesty?' Alice-Miranda asked.

He studied the picture. 'It is my Kiyomi.'

Alice-Miranda nodded. 'She was very lovely.'

'*Hai*. Kiko is so like her.'

The Emperor pulled a pocket watch from his suit jacket and flipped it open. Inside was a picture of his wife and a young girl, about four years of age.

'Is that Kiko?' Alice-Miranda asked.

The man nodded. 'Yes, she is a good daughter. But I have not been a good father.'

Alice-Miranda looked at the picture. She wondered why the girl's face seemed familiar.

At the other end of the table Hatsuko seethed. Her brother should have been wailing and sobbing and running from the room by now, as had happened so many times before. She despised his weakness and yet now that she was relying on it, he seemed to have gained new strength.

The Emperor stood up.

'Are you all right, Your Majesty?' Kenzo stood too and, like marionettes, everyone else was drawn to their feet.

'I would like my daughter to see this. In fact, it looks very much like one I gave her many years ago.'

'What are you doing?' Hatsuko flew to the end of the table.

'I am going to wake Kiko and bring her to dinner,' the man said.

'No, she is sick. You must not.' Hatsuko shook her head and reached out to grab his arm.

'Must? You will not command me, sister,' the Emperor hissed under his breath.

Hatsuko exhaled slowly and stood perfectly

still for a moment. The two siblings stared at each other.

'I . . . I will get her for you.' Hatsuko's face fell and she fled from the room.

Alice-Miranda looked at her father and mother, who shrugged.

'Please, our meal will be ruined.' Kenzo indicated that the group should sit down.

'I apologise for my sister. You see, we have not been together as a family for some time,' the Emperor said with a frown.

Dinner continued to be served in the princess's absence. Following the flower-like potato came the most exquisite sashimi, cut to resemble three-dimensional salmon with caviar for eyes. Millie poked at the dish and watched as everyone around her picked it up and swallowed it whole. She popped it into her mouth expecting it to be slimy, but was pleasantly surprised.

'This is *oishii*,' the girl exclaimed.

The Emperor smiled. 'I am glad it is to your liking, Miss Millie. And well done with your Japanese.'

Millie frowned. She hadn't used that word before and wondered how she even knew it.

The food continued coming. Next was *yakitori*

chicken and rice, then another dish with unidentifiable meat that no one was quite game to ask about.

Jacinta was squirming in her seat.

'What's the matter with you?' Millie whispered across the table.

'I need to go to the toilet,' Jacinta mouthed, then began jiggling up and down.

'Then go.' Millie flicked her head in the direction of the door.

Alice-Miranda noticed her friends' discomfort too. She slipped from her seat and walked to the end of the table.

'Excuse me, Kenzo-san,' she said quietly.

He leaned towards her.

'Could you tell me where the toilet is?'

'Certainly, Alice-Miranda.'

He held up his hand and a young woman walked forward. Then he said something to her in Japanese.

'Miki will show you,' he smiled at the child.

Alice-Miranda gestured to her friends. Jacinta stood up and, after a moment, Millie did too.

The three girls excused themselves and followed the young woman out of the room. They headed down a long hallway.

The woman pointed to a door on the left.

Jacinta charged through into a timber-lined room. There was another door leading to what looked like a giant powder room complete with an enormous vanity and two chairs. Yet another door led to the toilet.

'Whoa, if you thought the hotel toilet was cool, wait until you see this one,' Jacinta called out.

'Is it gold plated?' Millie asked through the door.

'No, but it has more controls than a jumbo jet.'

Alice-Miranda and Millie waited their turn inside the powder room while the woman who had led them there stood outside in the hallway.

'I was worried about the Emperor seeing my necklace,' Alice-Miranda said to Millie. 'When I met the old man in Obaasan's house, he told me that the woman in the photo was the Empress.'

'You didn't tell us that,' Millie said. 'That's pretty cool, you know. I wonder if it used to be owned by someone from the royal family.'

'I wondered that myself. I didn't think it was very likely but just now he said that it looked a lot like a necklace he gave Kiko.'

'He took it very well. He seems nice. Sad, but nice,' Millie said. 'I'm not so sure about his sister, though.'

'What do you mean?' Alice-Miranda asked.

'She's got this look, like she's up to something, and she seemed really unhappy to see her brother. I mean, I'd have thought she'd be pleased to see him up and about if he's been sick for such a long time.'

Alice-Miranda nodded. She had thought the same thing herself.

Jacinta was taking forever in the cubicle.

'What's that noise?' Millie asked, glancing around the room.

Alice-Miranda listened. Somewhere close by there were voices, and they didn't sound happy.

'Where are they coming from?' said Millie. She opened the door to the outer room but there was no one there. 'Must be coming through the paper walls or something,' Millie decided, then tapped her hand against the one closest. 'Ouch! Except that's not paper.'

The voices were getting louder.

Alice-Miranda and Millie looked at one another.

'It's coming from there,' Alice-Miranda whispered and pointed to the ground.

Millie knelt down and pressed her ear against the small silver drainage grate. 'I think it's Princess Hatsuko's voice.'

'What are you two whispering about?' Jacinta called from inside the toilet. 'You'd better not be talking about me and Lucas again.'

'Shhh,' Millie said.

Jacinta flushed the toilet and opened the door. 'What's the matter now?' she griped as she washed her hands.

'Listen,' Millie mouthed. The voices were speaking Japanese but Millie was shocked to realise that she could understand every word.

She listened to each sentence and translated aloud for Jacinta and Alice-Miranda. 'Princess Hatsuko is telling the man that the Emperor wants her to bring Princess Kiko into the dining room –'

'How do you know that's what she said?' Jacinta scoffed. 'They're speaking Japanese.'

'I don't know how, but I'm sure I'm understanding it perfectly. I just . . . am,' Millie whispered, looking as confused as Jacinta. 'Shh! They're still talking.'

Alice-Miranda's mind raced.

'Hatsuko's telling the man to put the letter – I don't know what letter – onto Kiko's bed.' Millie gasped. 'Oh my goodness – Kiko isn't even here! Hatsuko's going to wait a while then go back and tell everyone that's Kiko's run away . . .'

Alice-Miranda, Millie and Jacinta looked at one another, wide-eyed.

'Now Hatsuko's yelling at the man and telling him to find Kiko so they can use their original plan and take her to Kobe. Oh my goodness. Some law is changing tomorrow and Hatsuko's going to have Emperor Jimmu removed and take over the crown. That's it! She's trying to get rid of Princess Kiko so *she* can become Empress right away.'

Alice-Miranda couldn't keep quiet any longer. 'So where's Princess Kiko? Do you mean she's out in Tokyo all alone?'

Millie shushed her. 'Yes . . . *Oooh*. Hatsuko gave Kiko her grandfather's address to try to get her to run away. But the old man's not there – Hatsuko's saying she had him moved to some retirement home.' Millie gawped at the pendant around Alice-Miranda's neck. 'Hatsuko says that Kiko sold her necklace to the antique dealer in the Senso-ji market, Alice-Miranda! She's telling the man to ask the antique dealer if he remembers Kiko. Now the man's all excited and thinks he knows where Kiko is. That's weird. He's gabbling about some . . . about a boy in an alleyway in Asakusa. Hey, that's where we're staying.'

Shuffling noises came from the grate in the floor, followed by a loud bang.

'They're gone. How did I do that?' Millie said, stunned. 'How did I learn Japanese in two days? It's a miracle. Or I'm a genius and I just didn't know it.'

Alice-Miranda shook her head. 'I think I know how it happened. When you asked Mrs Oliver for a mint, what did she give you?'

Millie frowned. 'I don't know but it wasn't very minty. I wondered if she'd invented mint-less mints.'

'Oh my goodness, she gave you one of her language pills – she's just trialling them. That's why you can understand what they were saying.'

'Language pills? That's ridiculous,' Jacinta said.

Alice-Miranda shook her head. 'No, it's not. Mrs Oliver is one of the cleverest people I know and I promise it's true. She told me herself.'

Jacinta rolled her eyes and huffed. 'Why has she been keeping *that* to herself? It would have made life much easier since we've been here.'

'Because they're not ready yet. She took one and it sort of malfunctioned and she could only speak Japanese for the next few hours even though she was thinking in English.'

'I wonder if that will happen to me,' said Millie, biting her lip.

'And why isn't mine working?' Jacinta said. 'I had a mint too and I couldn't understand any of that.'

Alice-Miranda shrugged. 'I guess that's why they're still at the trial stage. Anyway, that's not important now. If what Millie said is true, Princess Kiko is in grave danger.'

'It sounds like she's planning to kill her,' Jacinta said.

'Or at the very least, lock her away forever,' Millie said.

'We have to tell the Emperor,' said Jacinta.

'No,' Alice-Miranda said. 'I think I know where she is too.' Alice-Miranda pictured the child in the photograph Emperor Jimmu had shown her.

'But how?' Millie frowned.

'Just trust me. We need to get there before those men do.'

Chapter 37

The girls sped out into the hallway, almost bowling Mrs Oliver over in the process.

'I wondered if you'd got lost in here,' the old woman said, smiling.

'Mrs Oliver, we have a problem. We need to talk to you – in private,' Alice-Miranda said. She'd just noticed that the young woman who had escorted them to the toilet was still waiting.

Millie walked over to the woman. 'Excuse us, you don't have to wait. Mrs Oliver can show us the way back,' she said in perfect Japanese.

'What was that, Millie?' Dolly frowned at the child. 'Oh my heavens, did you just speak Japanese?'

Alice-Miranda nodded. 'She's very good at it too.'

'In there. The lot of you. NOW!' Dolly pushed open the powder room door and the children rushed through.

'Millie took one of your tablets by mistake,' Alice-Miranda began.

Deep lines creased Dolly's forehead. 'But that's impossible!' She opened her handbag and fished around for the pill case. She pulled it out and then reached for her glasses. 'I know exactly how many of those tablets were in here. Now let me see, there were three of everything except the Japanese tablets – there were two of those left. Oh dear. And now there's only one.' The woman gulped. 'How on earth did that happen?'

'What about me? What did I take?' Jacinta asked anxiously.

'Not you too,' Dolly groaned. She counted the other pills. 'Well dear, I suspect you could be very good at Spanish in a little while.'

'*Gracias,*' Jacinta said. 'Oh, how exciting. I think it's started to take effect.'

'But how did you?' Dolly peered into the bag and pulled out a very similarly shaped case. 'The mints! Oh heavens, how utterly careless of me. I was so excited about coming to the palace, I wasn't paying attention. Girls, I am so sorry. I'm sure that you will be fine – in about seven hours.'

'Mrs Oliver, that's not the problem. We need your help. Can you get us to the inn?'

'Why on earth would we want to do that? We can't just leave, Alice-Miranda. It would be the height of rudeness.'

'I'm sure that we can explain to the Emperor and Mr Kenzo as soon as we find Princess Kiko and bring her safely home.'

'Find the princess? What are you talking about? What's she doing at the inn?' Dolly asked.

'Come on. We'll explain on the way.' Alice-Miranda grabbed Dolly's hand.

✻

Meanwhile, in the dining room, Kenzo glanced around at the empty chairs. He wondered what was taking everyone so long.

He motioned for the man behind him to step forward and whispered something into his ear.

'*Hai.*' The man scurried from the room to search for the missing guests and the princess.

'Dessert will soon be served,' Kenzo announced. 'Perhaps the children and Mrs Oliver have got lost out there somewhere.'

'It is a big place,' the Emperor agreed. 'One wrong turn and you could be gone for days.'

Hugh and Lawrence glanced across the table at one another. Hugh frowned. It wasn't like his daughter to take a wrong turn at all.

Chapter 38

'I'm driving this time,' Yuki yelled as he elbowed Yamato out of the way and scooted around to the other side of the vehicle. Their car was parked in the circular driveway behind the enormous limousine that had brought the guests to the palace.

Alice-Miranda, Millie, Jacinta and Mrs Oliver raced out of the palace. Alice-Miranda glanced towards the men as Yamato slid into the passenger seat and looked up. 'What are those children doing?' he said. 'And that old woman?'

Alice-Miranda looked at Millie in alarm. 'Hurry! Millie, please ask the driver if he can take us.'

'But I don't know how . . . Oh, of course, I do!' Millie thought about what she wanted to say then launched into near-perfect Japanese. She told the driver that she'd left something for the Emperor back at the inn and they needed to collect it before dinner was over. The driver opened the door and bowed.

She turned to Dolly. 'Mrs Oliver, you are the cleverest woman in the world! This is the best invention ever.'

The girls and Mrs Oliver piled into the back of the limousine. The driver pulled out in front of Yuki and Yamato, blocking their path.

Yuki leaned on the horn.

'Remember the men in black suits who were outside the inn? They're behind us,' Alice-Miranda said.

'What are they doing here?' Jacinta asked.

'Good heavens, young lady, what's been going on over there?' Dolly tutted.

Alice-Miranda tried to keep watch out the back window, but the black car behind them disappeared into the night. She had no idea if they were ahead or behind.

Jacinta was feeling very confused. 'So why are we going to the inn?'

'You know the boy who helped us with directions to the kimono maker?' Alice-Miranda explained.

Jacinta nodded. 'Yes, what about him?'

'He's not a boy!' Millie said, suddenly realising what Alice-Miranda already knew.

'How do you know that?' Jacinta asked.

'He's the princess, isn't he?' asked Millie.

'Yes, I'm sure of it,' Alice-Miranda said. 'Emperor Jimmu showed me a photograph of Princess Kiko in his fob watch. I was trying to remember why her face looked familiar and then when you explained that the men talking to Hatsuko said something about the inn and the alley, it all made sense. Do you remember that Yoshi seemed very interested in my pendant? I thought it was a bit odd for a boy to be so keen on jewellery. Yoshi is Kiko.'

'Do you think she sold the pendant?' Millie asked.

'Maybe. Or it might have been stolen,' said Alice-Miranda.

The limousine reached the inn in record time.

'Oh no, the men from the palace are already here,' Alice-Miranda said as she caught sight of the black car in front of Obaasan's.

'What are we going to do now?' Millie asked, leaning forward in her seat.

'What about you and Jacinta go to the front door and try to distract them, and I'll see if I can get in the side door and find the princess,' Alice-Miranda said.

'Right, good idea,' Millie nodded.

'What should I do, dear?' Mrs Oliver asked.

'I think you should take that last Japanese-language pill and see if you can get our driver to call the palace and let the Emperor know exactly what's going on.'

'Will do.' Dolly nodded decisively and opened her handbag. 'I just hope that it doesn't take too long to work. It seems to vary quite a bit.'

'Yes, my Spanish hasn't improved at all yet,' Jacinta said with a frown.

'Come on.' Alice-Miranda opened the back door and the three girls spilled out like a line of *kokeshi* dolls.

Millie and Jacinta ran towards the front of the house, while Alice-Miranda dashed into the alley.

She was about to knock on the side door when it opened and Yoshi peered out.

But this time Alice-Miranda knew better. 'Princess Kiko?'

The girl shook her head decisively. 'No! I don't know what you are talking about. I am Yoshi.' Kiko tried to close the door but Alice-Miranda shoved her foot inside.

'I know who you are and I'm afraid that you're in grave danger.' Alice-Miranda pushed the door and followed Kiko into the hall.

'Go away. You're not meant to be in here. It's none of your business,' Kiko implored her.

'Please, Princess, you must believe me. I've just come from the palace and those two men with the black car – the ones who were sitting in the alley all day – are at the front door now.'

Kiko gasped. She turned and crept down the hallway and then peered around the corner at the front door. A shadow loomed through the glass sidelights and the doorbell buzzed, followed by a thumping series of knocks. The colour drained from her cheeks.

'I'm not going back,' she whispered. 'They can't make me.'

'Taking you back is the last thing they want to do,' Alice-Miranda said. She looked closely at the girl and said carefully, 'Your aunt is plotting to get rid of you so she can become the Empress.'

'That is not true. Women cannot rule in Japan.'

'The laws are going to change tomorrow,' Alice-Miranda said.

'How do you know these things?' Kiko asked.

'It's a long story, but please believe me. I'm telling you the truth.'

'But I want to go to my grandparents. They will take care of me. I don't want to be a princess any more,' the child explained. 'My father doesn't want to see me and my aunt makes me study and hide in my room all day. She hates me. I want to be free, like Mari.'

'Who's Mari?' Alice-Miranda frowned.

'My songbird. I let her go so we could both be free.'

'Boy, where are you?' Obaasan's voice echoed through the house. 'I need some help in here. These old ladies want more tea – always more tea – we are drowning in tea.'

Alice-Miranda grabbed Kiko's hand and pulled her into the small bedroom Kiko had been using. 'You have to listen to me. We heard your aunt talking to those men. She is planning to have you imprisoned, or worse. She wants everyone to think that you have run away and can't be found. Then she is going to have your father declared incapable of ruling and she will become the Empress of Japan,' Alice-Miranda said.

'She was always hateful,' said Kiko sadly, 'but I never would have imagined she was capable of this.'

There was a shuffling sound outside the bedroom. Alice-Miranda began to speak but Kiko put a finger to her mouth.

A man said 'Hurry, Taro' in Japanese. Kiko recognised it as Tatsu, Obaasan's son.

'What are we doing?' the boy griped. The shuffling continued. It sounded as if something was being dragged along the hall.

'Getting rid of the evidence,' the man hissed.

'What did they say?' said Alice-Miranda.

Kiko translated.

'What evidence?' Alice-Miranda asked.

'But why?' the boy whined. 'It's heavy.'

'Because of that boy your grandmother let into the house. He has reported me to the authorities, I am sure of it. They have been watching us and now we must burn the papers or we will have to pay back all the money from the old people.'

'What old people?' Taro said.

'Are you that stupid, boy? The old people who live in this house and the ones who used to live here too.'

'Have you been collecting pension money for dead people?' Taro asked.

'Exactly!' The dragging noise continued.

'But isn't that against the law?' Taro said.

'It is not my fault that the law is weak, and I am smart,' Tatsu snarled. 'Wait until I get my hands on that boy. He will wish he never slept on our doorstep.'

The side door opened and the voices disappeared outside. Kiko translated this too. As she did, her eyes grew wide as she realised exactly what Tatsu's piles of papers were all about. 'He has been robbing the government. Collecting pensions from old people who lived here but who have died. I thought there was something strange about the birthdates on some of those forms. But I didn't tell anyone.' Kiko shook her head. 'I have enough troubles of my own.'

Kiko slid open the screen and peered out to see Taro dragging a large sack across the alley to the dumpster. His father was already standing there with another one.

Tatsu lit a match and threw it into the bin. After a moment, there was a *whump* and flames erupted from the top. Tatsu heaved the first sack into the fire, and then the second.

Kiko was distracted from this strange sight by a new voice coming from the front hall. This time it was deep and raspy and Kiko knew it immediately as one of her aunt's personal bodyguards.

'What do you want?' Obaasan was asking him.

'I'm looking for a child. A runaway.'

'What are you doing? Take off your shoes!' Obaasan demanded.

'Where are you hiding her – I mean, *him*?' The man's footsteps echoed on the timber floor.

'I don't need this. I am a busy woman. I have people to care for and Itoshii Squirrel to design. And I am tiiiiired. Yoshi, you come here now,' she yelled. Then she muttered under her breath, 'Looks like I am about to lose my best helper and I've only had him for a few days. What are you doing? He is not in the kitchen. Come back here!'

'Who's that?' Alice-Miranda asked.

'It is Yuki. He works for Aunt Hatsuko,' the child explained.

Alice-Miranda glanced out the back door into the alley. The fire in the dumpster was raging and Taro and his father were busy watching it.

'If we can get across to the inn, I'm sure we can hide there until the police come,' Alice-Miranda suggested.

'But my father doesn't want me. I have nothing to go back to.' Fat tears welled in Kiko's eyes.

'You're wrong about that. Your father loves you very much.' Alice-Miranda reached out and took the child's hands in hers.

Kiko wondered if that could be true. But there was something about this little girl that made Kiko want to believe it more than ever.

Outside, Jacinta and Millie had done their best to distract the two men in black who had come from the palace. Millie had intercepted them at the front door and asked a barrage of questions in her now perfect Japanese. At first the men seemed charmed by the child but a sharp buzzing in the taller man's ear refocused him on the task at hand. He told the other man to go around to the side door and make sure that Kiko didn't escape. The taller man had rung the doorbell until the old woman opened the door and he was able to force his way inside.

Alice-Miranda held Kiko's hand and together the girls made a dash for the back door but Alice-

Miranda stopped when she heard Millie's voice outside. She was speaking Japanese very loudly.

'That's my friend Millie out there,' Alice-Miranda whispered. 'What did she say?'

'She said that she had seen the boy who lives here run away down the alley earlier in the evening before you left to go to the palace.'

'We can't go that way. The other one of your aunt's men must be out there with her,' said Alice-Miranda. She grabbed Kiko's hand and they headed back along the hallway. Alice-Miranda peeked around the corner to check if it was safe to make a dash past the entrance hall. She was surprised to see Obaasan standing outside the kitchen door.

Obaasan turned around and saw the two girls.

Alice-Miranda raised her finger to her lips and shook her head.

Obaasan snorted but said nothing. Normally she would have handed the child over. But something wasn't right. She might not be able to see too well, but she knew trouble. And this tall man in her house had no respect. He didn't even remove his shoes and now he was in her kitchen making a mess.

The girls sped down the back hallway towards the stairs. 'Is there another way out?' Alice-Miranda whispered.

'I don't think so.'

'Is there somewhere we can hide?'

Kiko nodded. She grabbed Alice-Miranda's hand and ran up the stairs to the room at the end of the corridor. She tapped lightly on the door and poked her head around the corner.

'Hai?' Ojiisan looked at Kiko and beckoned for her to come in.

Alice-Miranda followed the older girl into the room. *'Arigatou,* Ojiisan. Please, may we stay here for a little while?'

The old man nodded. 'What is going on down there? Obaasan is screeching even more than usual.'

Downstairs, Yuki was striding through the house, turning the place upside down.

'Stop touching my things,' the old woman yelled. 'Look! The boy you are searching for has made a run for it.' She pointed towards the side door, which was slightly ajar.

Chapter 39

Yuki rushed out the door into the alley, almost bumping into Yamato, who was scratching his head with a bewildered look on his face.

'Where did she go?' Yuki demanded.

Yamato pointed to Millie, who was standing with Jacinta. 'That girl said that she saw the boy leaving the house with a backpack hours ago.'

'But the old woman said that she had just run away,' Yuki explained. 'Someone is lying.'

Jacinta pulled on Millie's kimono sleeve. 'Let's go and find Alice-Miranda.'

Millie shook her head. 'No. If we go inside they'll know that the princess is still there. We should wait until they leave.'

'Girls,' Mrs Oliver called as she caught sight of Millie and Jacinta. She'd been inside the limousine waiting for her tablet to take effect. Fortunately it had worked very quickly and she'd been able to explain to the driver exactly what was going on. The man had been visibly shocked and passed the telephone to Mrs Oliver, who had explained everything to Kenzo. At the moment she was having no trouble switching between English and Japanese.

Yuki and Yamato spun around as Mrs Oliver walked towards them.

'Your game is up,' she said calmly in Japanese. 'The authorities will be here any minute.'

'What are you talking about?' Yuki looked at Yamato and gulped. 'You're just a silly old woman.'

A sharp noise exploded in his eardrum. It was Hatsuko telling him much the same thing.

'Well, what are you waiting for?' Mrs Oliver could hear the woman's screeching through the earpiece. 'If I were you I'd get out of here quick smart.'

Millie nodded. 'Kidnapping a princess must be one of the worst crimes you can commit. I've heard that Japanese prisons are harsh places,' she said in Japanese.

'What are you two talking about?' Jacinta whined. 'I don't understand.'

Over by the dumpster, Tatsu and Taro were hiding as best they could and trying to work out exactly what was going on.

'Are those the men from the government?' Taro whispered to his father.

Tatsu shrugged. 'I'm not sure.'

'It sounds like they want Yoshi,' Taro said. 'Maybe you burned all the papers for no reason.'

His father clipped him over the ear. He had been thinking that too.

There was another hissing sound in Yuki's ear. The two men looked at each other. 'Let's go!' Yuki shouted.

He and Yamato ran towards their car and leapt in. The wheels spun as Yuki attempted to reverse down the narrow road. But his efforts were in vain as several cars sped towards him, blocking the car in. Yuki switched gears and drove forward, but between the limousine from the palace and another car which had entered the road from the other direction there was no escape.

✱

Back inside the house, the doorbell rang again.

'What now?' Obaasan called. 'What is going on around here?' The old woman shuffled along the back hall towards the front entrance. She opened the door and squinted.

'I beg your pardon, Obaasan.' A man dressed in a dinner suit bowed deeply. 'Please may I come in?'

The old woman wrinkled her nose and stared. She pulled her thick glasses from her apron pocket and put them on.

'Please let me introduce myself,' the man said.

Obaasan leaned forward. She looked up and tried her best to focus. 'Oh! It is not possible!' she gasped. 'What are you doing here?'

Chapter 40

The two girls huddled down beside Ojiisan's chair as far from the door as they could go.

'Please believe me,' Alice-Miranda said, as she looked into the princess's dark brown eyes. 'Your father does care for you. He came to dinner with us tonight. We didn't expect to see him at all but he looked so well and he talked about you and he wanted you to be with us.'

Ojiisan stared out the window into the street below. He had watched as two men in black suits argued in the alley. There was a fire raging in the dumpster bin too. But he was listening to the children next to him.

Kiko sniffed and said, 'It's my fault that my father's sick. He cannot stand to look at me. I remind him too much of my mother.'

Ojiisan picked up the leather-bound album and sat it on his knee. He opened it to the first page. Alice-Miranda glanced at it. She breathed in sharply and stared up at the old man. A knowing look settled on his face but he didn't say a word.

'How were you going to survive with no money and no one to care for you?' Alice-Miranda asked Kiko. 'Tokyo is a huge place and you're just a little girl.'

'I have my mother's diary. In it is an address for my grandparents. I thought if I could just find them, they would look after me. But I got lost and I ended up here. Obaasan is prickly but she is not unkind.'

'I thought the royal family all lived together at the palace,' Alice-Miranda said. 'Why weren't your grandparents there?'

'My mother was a commoner. When my father fell in love with her it caused many problems with his parents. They did not want him to marry outside of the royal circles and so my mother's parents were not invited to live at the palace. I asked Aunt Hatsuko and she said that my father would have nothing to do with them. But then I found my mother's diary and inside was their address. I wanted to find them. My mother wrote such beautiful words about her parents and I remember them just a little – I was only four when my mother was killed but I know she took me to see them once in their little house.'

Alice-Miranda looked over at the man. He'd closed his eyes and was clenching his hands. She reached up and took the album from Ojiisans's knee and passed it to the older girl. 'I think you have found your grandfather, Princess Kiko.'

Kiko stared at the first picture. 'That is my mother and my grandfather on my mother's wedding day.' She looked back at Alice-Miranda. 'How . . .?'

Ojiisan opened his eyes and brushed the moisture from his face. 'Kiko?' He bowed a little in his seat. 'I am right here.'

Kiko stood up. 'Ojiisan, is it really you?' She studied the man's face, then looked at the photograph.

'*Hai*, it is me. I am a very old man now but that is me in the photograph. I should have known when I saw those hands of yours. But you always hid your face.'

Kiko took off her cap and looked at the man.

'You have your mother's eyes.'

The child reached forward and embraced him. He kissed her forehead and held her as tightly as he could.

Alice-Miranda smiled and swept a tear from her own eye.

Outside in the hallway there were voices.

Kiko stepped back. 'Please, Ojiisan, don't let Aunt Hatsuko's men take me away.'

The door opened and Kiko looked up. She felt as if the breath had been sucked from her body.

'Kiko.'

'Father,' she whispered.

'You are safe now. I know all about my sister's plans. She cannot hurt you any more.' The Emperor rushed over and scooped her into his arms. 'I am so sorry – please forgive me. I have been a terrible father. My heart has been so heavy with guilt. It was my fault that your mother died. I was careless and I almost killed you too.' He reached out to touch the scar on her face.

'But Father, I am alive. I need you. I've needed

you for so many years.' Tears began to fall down Kiko's cheeks.

'And I realise now how much I need you too, my daughter. Please forgive me.' He pressed his lips against her forehead.

Obaasan shuffled to the door and watched as best she could the scene playing out in front of her.

Millie, Jacinta and Mrs Oliver had let themselves in the side door and made their way upstairs. They were standing behind Obaasan and peering into the room too.

The Emperor put his daughter back down and looked at the old man. 'My goodness, is it really you? Father-in-law?'

The old man nodded slowly.

'But how? Oh, I remember . . . I was very sick. Hatsuko was being so kind and helping look after my affairs. Or so I thought until tonight. She came to tell me that you and your wife had died. It was another sadness I could not bear,' the Emperor explained.

'It is true my beloved wife has passed away. After that, some officials from the palace came to my home and insisted that it had been arranged for me to live here. I am too old to manage on my own. It was a kind gesture to look after me but I was always sad that my letters to you and Kiko were returned,' the old man explained.

Kiko and her father shook their heads. There had never been any letters.

Obaasan wrinkled her nose and peered into the room. 'Do you mean to tell me that my good boy Yoshi is a princess and this Ojiisan is the princess's grandfather?'

Alice-Miranda nodded.

'*Hai,*' the Emperor said.

'And the Emperor of Japan is in my house. What is going on around here? I am just an old woman with a crazy flying squirrel and lots of *really* old people to look after.'

The two girls smiled at each other.

'I think we should be getting home,' the Emperor said.

Ojiisan nodded. 'Perhaps you will come and see me sometime, my granddaughter.'

'No,' said the Emperor. He shook his head emphatically.

Kiko's eyes welled with tears. 'But Father, please.'

'You will not have to come and visit Ojiisan,

Kiko, because Ojiisan is coming to live with us where he should always have been.'

Alice-Miranda clapped her hands with delight. 'That's wonderful news.'

Kiko embraced her father then her grandfather.

'And if it weren't for you, I don't know where I might have ended up.' Kiko smiled at Alice-Miranda and hugged her too. The child caught sight of Mrs Oliver, Millie and Jacinta in the hallway.

'You can thank Mrs Oliver, really. It was her new invention that saved the day.'

Kiko frowned. 'Invention?'

Alice-Miranda opened her mouth, then closed it again for a moment. 'Never mind. I'm just glad that we found you.' She reached up and undid the clasp on her locket. She pulled it out from under the collar of her kimono. 'I think this belongs to you.'

Kiko shook her head and closed Alice-Miranda's palm around the locket. 'No. It is yours. You have given me something much more precious than that.' She smiled at her father and grandfather. Alice-Miranda reached out and the two children embraced again.

'Oh great, now I have to find someone else for Ojiisan's room,' Obaasan grouched. 'Always work to do, phone calls, squirrels . . . and who are you people?' She looked at Mrs Oliver and Millie and Jacinta. 'Maybe I am getting too ooooooold for all this,' she sputtered to herself as she shuffled away down the hall.

Alice-Miranda giggled. The princess did too.

And just in case you're wondering . . .

That night, Princess Kiko returned to the palace with her father and grandfather. It seemed that her grandfather's letters had been intercepted by Princess Hatsuko as part of her grand plan to seize power from her brother and get rid of her niece. She had always resented the fact that, although she was the eldest sibling, because she was a woman she would never rule. When there were moves afoot to change the law so that Kiko would inherit the crown, Hatsuko saw her opportunity. She had found the Empress's diary and planted it in Kiko's room. She knew that when the child found her grandparents' address, she would want to search for them. After all, her life in the palace was such a miserable one. Hatsuko had made it easy to run away. She ensured that staff were off-duty, doors were open and gates unlocked. She never intended to kill the child, but she had set up what amounted to a prison in an abandoned castle in a remote part of Kobe.

The Emperor was horrified to learn of his sister's intentions and the evil treatment of his only child. He vowed that Hatsuko's life would now be equally unpleasant and decided that rather than lock her away, as she would have done to Kiko, she should be made to do something useful in society. She was appointed as Obaasan's new live-in assistant – with strict instructions that the old woman keep her under lock and key. Yuki and Yamato and their technical friend found themselves reassigned too – to the city's waste management team.

Kenzo was heartbroken to learn that the woman he loved could be so cruel. The torch that he had carried for her for many years was well and truly extinguished, and he resigned himself to the fact that he would most likely be a bachelor for the rest of his days. Hugh disagreed with his friend. As he pointed out, there were at least a couple of hundred single young women working in the palace who might be very interested in the particularly handsome Grand Chamberlain.

It turned out that Obaasan had been completely unaware of her son's fraudulent activities. While it was true that she collected old people to live in her house, her son deliberately neglected to report any of their deaths to the authorities and continued to collect their pension money for years afterwards. Obaasan thought she had a safe full of cash because her Itoshii Squirrel business was booming. Sadly, that was just a front for Tatsu to launder the money. Tatsu was wrong about anyone reporting him. It seems he had become increasingly paranoid about being caught and with the appearance of police cars and men in black sitting in the alley, he brought himself unstuck in the end. Tatsu was forced to pay the money back to the government. The judge decided he should be kept under house arrest with Obaasan in charge of him – after all, she could inflict much more pain than any prison.

Obaasan's dreams of a giant Itoshii Squirrel seemed thwarted until the Emperor decided to commission the creature in recognition of her kindness to his father-in-law and daughter. A two-metre tall squirrel in aviation goggles now stands proudly at the entrance to the Senso-ji Temple arcade.

Hugh Kennington-Jones decided that Dolly's language pill development was one of the most exciting things he'd ever heard about. But it had to remain top-secret until they could be sure that there were no strange side effects. Millie enjoyed her night being able to speak Japanese and couldn't wait until the pills were available for regular use. Jacinta, on the other hand, was sorely disappointed that her Spanish never got past a few words.

Princess Kiko invited the children back to the palace to thank them for everything they had done. They had a wonderful time exploring, and when Alice-Miranda opened her locket and pulled out the photograph of the Empress for Kiko to keep, she discovered the tracker. At once, it became clear why Yuki and Yamato had been following the wrong child. Princess Kiko took the little device and threw it into one of the palace ponds, where a giant koi carp rose to the surface and swallowed it in one gulp.

As the girls wandered through the garden, they could hear warbling birdsong. A little yellow canary landed on a branch of a cherry blossom tree. It seemed that Kiko wasn't the only one who had come home.

Cast of characters

Highton-Smith-Kennington-Jones household, family and friends

Alice-Miranda Highton-Smith-Kennington-Jones	Only child, eight and one-quarter years old
Cecelia Highton-Smith	Alice-Miranda's mother
Hugh Kennington-Jones	Alice-Miranda's father
Dolly Oliver	Family cook, part-time inventor
Mrs Shillingsworth	Head housekeeper
Aunt Charlotte Highton-Smith	Cecelia's younger sister
Lawrence Ridley	Aunt Charlotte's husband and a famous actor
Lucas Ridley	Lawrence's son
Millicent Jane McLoughlin-McTavish-McNoughton-McGill	Alice-Miranda's best friend
Jacinta Headlington-Bear	Friend

Pippa McLoughlin-McTavish	Millie's mother
Hamish McNoughton-McGill	Millie's father
Ambrosia Headlington-Bear	Jacinta's mother

Others

Aki	Hotel receptionist
Kiko	Runaway eleven-year-old
Hatsuko	Kiko's aunt
Jimmu	Kiko's father
Yuki and Yamato	Hatsuko's assistants
Michiko	Fashion designer in Harajuku
Obaasan	An old woman
Tatsu	Obaasan's son
Taro	Tatsu's son
Kenzo Aoki	Old student friend of Hugh's
Professor Dimble	An inventor
Nobu Taguchi	Representative from the Japanese Ministry for Invention and Innovation

Look out for Alice-Miranda's
amazing **tenth** adventure

Coming 1 September 2014

Loved the book?

There's so much more
stuff to check out online

AUSTRALIAN READERS:

randomhouse.com.au/kids

NEW ZEALAND READERS:

randomhouse.co.nz/kids